BANDIT COUNTRY

SAS
OPERATION

Bandit Country

PETER CORRIGAN

HARPER

Harper
An imprint of HarperCollins*Publishers*
1 London Bridge Street,
London SE1 9GF
www.harpercollins.co.uk

This paperback edition 2016
1

First published by 22 Books/Bloomsbury Publishing plc 1995

Copyright © Bloomsbury Publishing plc 1995

Peter Corrigan asserts the moral right to
be identified as the author of this work

A catalogue record for this book
is available from the British Library

ISBN: 978 0 00 815539 1

Set in Sabon by Born Group using Atomik ePublisher from Easypress

Printed and bound in Great Britain

This book is respectfully dedicated to the officers and men of C Company, 4th/5th Battalion the Royal Irish Rangers

Prologue

South Armagh, 3 July 1989
The foot patrol moved quietly down the starlit street. There were four of them, forming a 'brick'. They made up a single fire team. The point man kept his SA-80 assault rifle in the crook of his shoulder, eyes glinting in his darkly camouflaged face as he scanned surrounding windows, doors and alleyways.

Behind the point came the fire team's commander, a corporal. Hung on the left side of his chest was a PRC 349 radio. It had a range of only a few kilometres, but the patrol was not far from home. The corporal had the 349 set on whisper mode. Its twin microphones were strapped to his throat and he edged a finger in between them, silently cursing the way they irritated his skin.

Behind the corporal came the gunner, armed with a Light Support Weapon. Similar to an SA-80, it had a longer barrel and a bipod to steady it.

The rear man was walking backwards, checking the street the patrol had just walked through. The men were in staggered file, two on each side of the road, covering each other as they made their way back to the safety of the Security Forces Base. It was pitch-dark, and they avoided the few street-lights that still worked in that part of the village. All of them had the needle in the sights of their weapons turned on so that it was a luminous line, helping them to pick out targets at night.

They were near the centre of the village now. The locals had whitewashed all the walls so that a patrolling soldier would stand out more clearly against them. That was the worst part.

A dog barked, and they all paused to listen, hunkering down in doorways. Nothing worse than a restless fucking dog; it told the locals they had visitors.

The barking stopped. The corporal waved a hand and they were on their way again.

The centre of Crossmaglen had a small, open square. Crossing it was the most dangerous part of any patrol. It had to be done quickly as the whitewashed house walls offered no concealment. As the brick paused on the edge of the square the point man looked back at his commander. The corporal nodded and took up a firing position, as did the other two men.

The point man set off across the square at a sprint. He was halfway across when there was a sharp crack, startlingly loud in the still night air. The point man seemed to be knocked backwards. He fell heavily on to his back and then lay still.

For a second the rest of the fire team was frozen, disbelieving. Then the corporal began shouting.

'Sniper! Anyone see the flash?'

'Not a fucking thing, Corp.'

'Ian's out there – we've got to go and get him! Gunner, set up the LSW for suppressive fire. Mike, we're going to run out there and bring him in, OK?'

When the gunner was on the ground, with the LSW's stock in his shoulder, the other two soldiers dashed out into the open.

Immediately there was the sound of automatic fire. Tarmac was blown around their legs as the bullets thumped down around them. The point man lay in a pool of shining liquid. His chest looked as though someone had broken it open to have a look inside. Behind them, the LSW gunner opened up on automatic. Suddenly the little square was deafening with the sound of gunfire. Red streaks sped through the air and ricocheted off walls: the tracer in the LSW magazine. A series of flashes came from an alleyway opening off the square, and there was the unmistakable bark of an AK47, somehow lighter than the single shot that had felled the point man.

'Come on, Mike. Grab his legs.'

'He's dead, Corp!'

'Grab his fucking legs, like I tell you!'

They staggered back across the square with their comrade's body slung between them like a sack. The firing had stopped. All around, lights were flicking on at windows. There was the sound of doors banging.

'Get a fucking field-dressing on him, Mike. Gunner, did you see where that bastard is?'

'Saw the muzzle flash, Corp. But I think he's bugged out now. The locals will be all over us in a minute though.'

The corporal swore viciously, then thumbed the pressel-switch of the 349.

'Hello, Zero, this is Oscar One One Charlie. Contact, over.'

The far-away voice crackled back over the single earphone.

'Zero, send over.'

'One One Charlie, contact 0230, corner of . . .' – the corporal looked round wildly – 'corner of Hogan's Avenue and Cross square. One own casualty, at least two enemy with automatic weapons. I think they've bugged out. Request QRF and medic for casevac, over.'

'Roger, One One Charlie. QRF on its way, over.'

'Roger out.'

The corporal bent over his injured point man. 'How is he, Mike?'

The other soldier was ripping up field-dressings furiously and stuffing them into the huge chest wound.

'Fucking bullet went right through his trauma plate, Corp – right fucking through and went out the other side. What the hell kind of weapon was that?'

The soldiers all wore flak-jackets, and covering their hearts front and rear were two-inch-thick 'trauma plates' of solid Kevlar. These stopped most normal bullets, even those fired by a 7.62mm Kalashnikov AK47.

'It's that bastard sniper. He got us again.' The corporal was livid with fury. 'The bastard did it again,' he repeated.

There was a loud banging in the night, the metallic clatter of dustbin lids being smashed repeatedly on the ground. Crossmaglen's square was filling up with people.

The sound of engines roaring up other streets. A siren blaring. The flicker of blue lights. A Quick Reaction Force was on its way.

'He's gone, Corp. Poor bugger never had a chance.'

Armoured Landrovers, both green and slate-grey, powered into the square, scattering the approaching mob. The locals were shouting and cheering now – they had seen the little knot of men on the corner, the body on the ground. They knew what had happened.

'Nine-nil, nine-nil, nine-nil,' they chanted, laughing. Even when baton-wielding soldiers and RUC men poured out of the Landrovers to force them back, they continued jeering.

'Nineteen years old,' the corporal said. 'His first tour. Jesus Christ.'

He closed the blood-filled eyes of the boy on the ground. The Border Fox had struck again.

1

'What do you have that I can use?' Lieutenant Colonel Blair asked, sipping his coffee.

Brigadier General Whelan, Commander of Land Forces in Northern Ireland, looked at his subordinate warily.

'I can give you an additional Special Support Unit from 39 Brigade's patch,' he replied.

'RUC cowboys? But sir, I've lost four men in four months, all to the same sniper. Morale is rock-bottom, and the local players know it. I've already had three complaints this week alone. The boys are taking it out on the population.'

Whelan held up a hand and said: 'This is a bad time of year, Martin. The marching season is almost upon us. We're overstretched, and Whitehall won't hear of us bringing in another battalion.'

'It's not another battalion we need. I was thinking of something more compact.'

'The Intelligence and Security Group?'

'Yes. To be frank, sir, we're getting nowhere. Our own Covert Observation Platoon has drawn a series of blanks. I don't have the resources within my own patch to tackle this problem. We need outside help – and I'm talking help from our own people, not the RUC.'

'Hasn't E4 come up with anything?'

'Special Branch guards its sources like an old maid her virginity. They're terrified of compromising the few touts they have. No – we need a new approach. This South Armagh Brigade is the tightest-knit we've ever encountered. It's better even than the Mid-Tyrone one was a few years back. The Provos seem to have taken the lessons of Loughgall to heart. They're very slick, and they've recovered amazingly quickly. This Border Fox now has up to three ASUs operating in close support. We need to take out not only him, but at least one of those back-up units.'

'Take out? You rule out more conventional methods of arrest, then?'

'I believe it would be too risky. No, this bastard is fighting his own little war down near the border. The South Armagh lot need to have the carpet pulled out from under them.'

'And your men need a kill.'

Lieutenant Colonel Blair, commanding officer of 1st Battalion the Royal Green jackets, paused.

'Yes, they do.' He would not have been so open with any other senior officer, but Whelan was a member of the 'Black Mafia' himself – an ex-Greenjacket who had done his stint as CO of a battalion in South Armagh.

'This is irregular, Martin – you know that. You're asking me to initiate an operation in a vacuum. Usually it is the Tasking and Coordinating Group that comes to me . . .'

'More Special Branch,' said Blair with a wave of his hand. 'This is not an RUC problem. It is the Green Army that is taking the casualties, my men that are out there in the bogs day after day and night after night, while the RUC conduct vehicle checkpoints and collar drink-drivers.'

Whelan was silent. It was true that the uniformed 'Green Army' had been paying a heavy price lately for the patrolling of the border, or 'Bandit Country' as the men on the ground called it. And the Border Fox had made headlines both in the UK and America. He was a hero to the Nationalist population and their sympathizers across the Atlantic. Nine members of the Security Forces had been killed by him in the last eighteen months, the last only a few days ago. All of them had been killed by a single bullet from a high-calibre sniper rifle that had punched through the men's body armour as though it were cardboard. The capture of that weapon, more importantly, the termination of the Fox's activities, were obviously desirable.

But Whelan did not like authorizing what were in effect assassinations. He had no moral qualms about the issue – the Fox had to be stopped, and killing him was an effective way of doing that. But he hated giving the Republican Movement yet another martyr. Political consideration had to be taken into account also. If he authorized an op against the Fox he would have to inform the Secretary of State – in guarded terms of course – of what was about to happen.

More importantly, there was the feasibility of the operation. Intelligence in 3 Brigade's Tactical Area of Responsibility was poor. The IRA brigade in South Armagh seemed very tightly knit and so far all attempts to cultivate informers had failed. It was impossible to proceed without good intelligence, and seemingly impossible to obtain that intelligence. Hence the Security Forces were powerless, for all their helicopters and weapons. And so the Fox continued his killing unhindered, which was why he had Martin Blair in his office, seething with baffled anger.

'Damn it, Martin, don't you think I see your point? But how can we proceed with anything when we have nothing to go on? Special Branch has drawn a blank, and your own covert op has turned up nothing.'

'Then we must create our own intelligence', Blair said doggedly.

'What do you mean?'

'Give me the Int and Sy Group. Let them loose in my patch. They may turn up something.'

'That's a hell of a vague notion.'

'They're doing bugger-all at the moment except interminable weapons training. I got that from James Cordwain himself. The rest of the Province is as quiet as the grave.'

Whelan winced at his subordinate's choice of words. Major Cordwain was OC of the combined Intelligence and Security Group and 14 Intelligence Company. 'Int and Sy', or more often just 'The Group', was another name for Ulster Troop, the only members of the SAS who were based permanently in the Province. Fourteen Intelligence Company was another pseudonym for a crack surveillance unit drawn from all units in the army and trained by the SAS themselves.

'Int and Sy's job description does not include charging in like the bloody cavalry, guns blazing.'

Colonel Blair smiled. 'Tell James Cordwain that.'

'Indeed.' Cordwain had taken over the Group less than a year ago. He and his young second in command, Lieutenant Charles Boyd, were a pair of fire-eaters. Cordwain had been with 22 SAS in the Falklands and was an expert in covert surveillance and the tricky business of so-called 'Reactive Observation Posts' – known to the rest of the army as Ambushes.

'You've spoken to Cordwain about this, then?' Whelan asked sharply. He did not like officers, even fellow Greenjackets, who flouted the chain of command.

Blair stiffened. 'Yes, sir, I did – informally of course.'

'And what was his reaction?'

'He thought he might have a way in.'

'What is it?'

'An operative of ours, based in Belfast at the moment. He used to be part of Int and Sy but MI5 have become his handlers. Been here for over a year, and has a perfect cover.'

'His name?'

'Cordwain wouldn't say. But he thinks it would be possible to relocate him, weasel him into the South Armagh lot.'

'He must be an exceptional man.'

'Actually, Cordwain says he's one of the best he's ever seen. Parents were from Ballymena, so he has the perfect accent for starters. They were in the South Atlantic together.'

Whelan got up, crossed the office to the sideboard and the decanter that stood there. He poured out two whiskies into Waterford-crystal tumblers and offered one to Blair.

'Bushmills – the Irish. Bloody good stuff.'

They drank. Whelan looked out of his office window, past the ranks of Landrovers and Saxon armoured personnel carriers, over to where the perimeter wall rose high with netting and razor-wire; it was supposed to intercept RPG 7 missiles or Mark 12 mortars, the Provos' current flavour of the month.

'We are skating on thin ice here, Martin,' Whelan said.

'Yes, sir, I know. But my men are dying.'

'Yes. But MI5, they're tighter with their operatives than E4 is with its information. They may not want to let us play with this man.'

'Cordwain thinks it may be possible to bypass MI5, sir.'

Whelan spun round. 'Does he now? And how would we do that?'

'This man, he has a personal reason for wanting to see the Border Fox brought in. One of my young subalterns was a relative of his.'

'Ah yes, I remember. That was tragic, Martin, tragic. So it's revenge this man wants. That may not make him totally reliable.'

'Cordwain seems to think he is, sir, and Boyd, his 2IC, is willing to provide back-up.'

Whelan set down his glass and leaned over the desk until his face was close to Blair's.

'You seem to have thought this out with unusual thoroughness, Colonel.'

'Yes, sir.'

'I am not used to being given fully-fledged covert operational plans by my battalion commanders. Is that clear, Colonel?'

'Perfectly, sir.'

Whelan straightened.

'It may be we will be able to keep this under an army hat. I would certainly prefer it that way – and you say that Special Branch can give us nothing. But we must be even more discreet than usual – and I am not talking about the Paddies, Colonel. I will speak to Cordwain. I will give him the necessary authorization . . .' As Blair brightened, Whelan frowned thunderously and cut him off.

'But mark me, Martin, this conversation never took place. This man of Cordwain's will be disowned by every security agency in the Province if he so much as sniffs of controversy. And Cordwain's back-up will be on their own also. If the press – or God help us the Minister – ever find out about this we'll be crucified.'

'I understand, sir.'

'Be sure that you do, Martin.' The General tossed off the last of his Bushmills with practised ease. Now you'll have to go, I'm afraid. I have a bloody cocktail party to go to. I have to rub noses with the Unionists and win some hearts and minds.'

10

2

Belfast

The Crown Bar, opposite the much-bombed Europa Hotel, was quiet. It was two o'clock on a weekday afternoon and there seemed to be only a handful of men in there, seated in the walled-off snugs and nursing Guinness or whiskey, leafing through the *Belfast Telegraph*.

One of those men was Captain John Early of the SAS. He was a squat, powerful figure of medium height who appeared shorter because of the breadth of his shoulders. He could have – and frequently did – pass for a brickie on his lunch hour or whiling away the days of unemployment. His hands were blunt and calloused, the arms powerfully muscled. His face was square, the close-cropped hair sprinkled with premature grey at the temples and a badly broken nose making him look slightly thuggish. But the blue eyes were intelligent, belying the brutality of the face. Despite the haircut, he did not look like a soldier, certainly not a holder of the Queen's Commission. And when he quietly asked the barman for another pint his accent bore the stamp of north-east Ulster.

There was no trace left of the clean-cut young officer who had joined the Queen's Regiment back in 1977, or even of the

11

breezy subaltern who had agonized through SAS selection eight years previously. Turnover of officers among the SAS was much swifter than that of troopers; they rarely served more than five or six years with a Sabre Squadron. Early had come over with Ulster Troop in 1984 and gone undercover two years later. He was an 'independent', operating now under the aegis of MI5, but he never forgot where he had come from. If he died here, his name would be inscribed on the Clock Tower in Hereford, where all the dead of the SAS left their names.

Early sipped his whiskey patiently. He was waiting for a friend.

James Cordwain came through the door. Early recognized him instantly, though he hadn't seen him in years. The hair was longer of course – all the SAS seemed to believe that long hair was obligatory when serving in Northern Ireland. But he still had the aristocratic bearing, the finely chiselled jaw and flashing eyes. He looked every inch an officer. Early sighed, ordered another drink and took it into a snug.

It was ten minutes before Cordwain joined him, smiling.

'You're not an easy man to get hold of, John.'

'The name is Dominic, Dominic McAteer,' Early told him sharply. Cordwain winced.

'Why did we have to meet anyway? A phone call could have done it.'

Cordwain shook his head, regaining his self-assurance quickly. 'I had to talk to you in person.'

'Talk then.'

Cordwain looked at him, slightly offended. They had been good friends once, in the Falklands. Early seemed aged, irritable beyond his years. It was undercover work that did it, Cordwain decided.

'I have a Q car down the street. We can talk in there,' he said. A Q car was the army's name for an unmarked vehicle.

'Are you mad? Every dicker in the city knows a Q car when he sees one. We're safe enough here. I know the barman. He thinks I'm just another unemployed navvy and you're in here about a job.'

'Which, in a way, I am.'

'So tell me about it.'

Cordwain tried hard not to look smug. 'It's on.'

'When?'

'As soon as you can relocate. We have an opening down in Cross. Construction.'

'Not on a fucking army base, I trust.'

Cordwain grinned. 'Not likely. No, a local firm, Lavery's, has been given a contract – new bungalows.'

Early's eyes narrowed. 'It's a front, is it?'

'Yes and no. The contract is real enough, but our people are the ones behind it, buried three layers deep. Get yourself settled in, and then we'll start working on a channel of communication.'

'I take it Special Branch came up with fuck-all.'

'They don't even know you exist.'

Early nodded. He liked it that way.

'What about our friends the spooks?' he said, referring to his handlers in the Intelligence Service.

'You're on leave, seeing a sick auntie. They think you're back across the water. They'll be mightily pissed off when the truth comes out though.'

'Fuck them. This is my last caper, James. After this I'm getting out.'

'I'm sorry about Jeff. I take it he's the reason behind all this.'

Jeffrey Early had hero-worshipped John and gone into the army as soon as he could, following in his revered older

13

brother's footsteps. But the Border Fox had killed Jeff three months ago. One bullet, taking off most of his head. Early had not even been able to go to the funeral.

'I want this bastard, James. I really want him.'

Cordwain nodded. 'Don't let hatred cloud your thinking, John. Remember, your job will be identification. I provide the Button Men.'

'Who are they?'

'Charles Boyd for one. You don't know him, but he's a good man.'

'I don't want him tripping over my shadow, James. This South Armagh lot are the most formidable we've ever encountered. They sniff the colour green and I'm dead. Tell your man to keep his distance.'

Cordwain was not happy. 'They have to provide effective back-up.'

'So long as they don't compromise me.'

'They won't. I'll have a word. Boyd will want to meet you as soon as is practicable.'

'Why, for fuck's sake?'

'To get a feel of the thing. He wants you to draw him a few pictures.'

'Are you saying he's still wet behind the ears?'

Cordwain grinned. 'A little. He's out in west Tyrone at the minute, but that op should finish within a day at most.'

'Terrific.' Early finished his drink and stood up, glancing quickly over the wooden partition of the snug. The bar was still more or less deserted.

'I'll be in touch.'

Then he left, exchanging a farewell with the barman as he went. Cordwain lingered a while to leave a gap between them. This had to be the most hare-brained operation he had ever begun. But the men Upstairs had given the go-ahead, and besides, he did not like doing nothing while British soldiers were slaughtered with impunity. Talking once to an officer in the 'Green Army', he had been struck by a phase the man had used. 'We're just figure 11s, out standing on the streets,' the officer had said. A 'figure 11' was the standard target used on firing ranges. Cordwain did not like the image. It was time the terrorists took a turn at ducking bullets.

Lieutenant Charles Boyd shifted position minutely to try to get some blood circulating in his cramped and chilled legs. The rain had been pouring down for hours now, reducing visibility and soaking him to the marrow. There were streams of freezing water trickling down the neck of his combat smock and between his buttocks. He was lying in a rapidly deepening puddle with the stock of an Armalite M16 assault rifle close to his cheek. His belt-order dug into his slim waist and his elbows were sinking deeper into peat-black mud.

'July in Tyrone,' his companion whispered. 'Jesus fucking Christ. Why didn't I become a grocer?'

'Shut it, Haymaker.'

'Yes, boss,' the other man mumbled. The hissing downpour of the rain reduced the chances of their being heard but there was no point in taking risks.

It was getting on towards evening; the second evening they had spent in the observation post. They were screened by a tangle of alder and willow; behind them a stream gurgled, swollen by the rain. Their camouflaged bergens rested between their ankles.

They had not moved in thirty-six hours. Boyd began to wonder if the SB had been wrong. He had been tasked to provide a Reactive Observation Post to monitor an arms cache which was to have been visited last night, but no one had shown. The cache was at the base of a tree eighty metres away – they could see it plainly even with the rain. The local ASU, an IRA Active Service Unit of four men, was planning a 'spectacular' for the forthcoming Twelfth of July marches. Boyd and his team were to forestall them, and had been discreetly given the go-ahead to use all necessary means to achieve that aim. To Boyd that meant only one thing: any terrorist who approached this cache was going to die. It would give the Unionists something to crow about on their holiday and sweeten relations between them and the Northern Ireland Office. Boyd didn't give a shit about either, but he wanted to nail this ASU. They had been a thorn in 8 Brigade's flesh for some months now, though they were not as slick as their colleagues in Armagh.

Lying beside Boyd was Corporal Kevin 'Haymaker' Lewis, so called because of his awesome punch. It was rumoured he had killed an Argie in the Falklands with one blow of his fist. Haymaker was an amiable man, though built like a gorilla. He had the tremendous patience and stamina of the typical SAS trooper, but he loved grousing.

Hidden some distance to the rear of the pair were Taff Gilmore and Raymond Chandler. All troopers seemed to have some nickname or other. Taff was so called not because he was Welsh but because he had a fine baritone voice which he exercised at every opportunity. And Raymond – well, what else could the lads call someone with the surname Chandler? Some of them, though, called him 'The Big Sleep' because of his love of his sleeping bag.

It was unusual for an officer to accompany an op such as this. SAS officers had on the whole stopped accompanying the other ranks into the field since the death of Captain

Richard Westmacott in 1980, gunned down by an M60 machine-gun in Belfast's Antrim Road. But Boyd loved working in the field – not for him the drudgery of the ops room in some security base. He knew that the men called him 'our young Rupert' behind his back, but he also knew that they respected him for his decision.

God, the bloody rain, the bloody mud, the bloody Provos. The players, as the Army termed the key terrorist figures, were probably warm and safe in their houses. Not for them the misery of this long wait in the rain, the pissing and shitting into plastic bags, the cold tinned food.

Boyd felt Haymaker tense beside him. His mind had been wandering. The big trooper looked his officer in the eye, then nodded out at the waterlogged meadow with its straggling hedgerows. There was movement out there in the rain, a dark flickering of shadow close to the hedge. Immediately Boyd's boredom and weariness disappeared. The evening was darkening but it was still too light to use Night Vision Goggles, which made the darkest night into daylight. He squinted, his fist tightening round the pistol-grip of the M16. One thumb gently levered off the safety-catch. The weapon had been cocked long ago, the magazine emptied and cleaned twice in the past thirty-six hours. The M16 was a good weapon for a nice heavy rate of fire, but it was notoriously prone to jamming when dirty.

Boyd's boot tapped Haymaker on the ankle. He gave the thumbs down, indicating that the enemy was in sight. Haymaker grinned, rain dripping off his massive, camouflaged face, and sighed down the barrel of his own Armalite. Boyd could hear his own heartbeat thumping in his ears.

Two men were walking warily up the line of the hedge. This had to be it – who else would be tramping the fields on such a shitty evening? Boyd forced himself to remember the mugshots of the key Tyrone players. Would it be Docherty? Or McElwaine?

The men had stopped. Boyd cursed silently. Had they been compromised? Besides him, Haymaker was like a great, wet statue. The pair of them hardly dared breathe.

They were moving again, thank Christ. Boyd could see them clearly now, buttoned up in parkas, their trousers soaked by the wet grass. McElwaine and the youngster, Conlan.

The two IRA men stopped at the tree which marked the cache, looked around again, and then bent to the ground and began rummaging in the grass. One of them produced a handgun with a wet glint of metal. They were pulling up turves, their fingers slipping on the wet earth.

Should he initiate the ambush now? No. Boyd wanted a 'clean' kill – he wanted both terrorists to have weapons in their hands when he opened up. That way there would be no awkward questions asked afterwards. The 'yellow card', the little document all soldiers in the Province carried, specified that it was only permitted to open fire without warning if the terrorist was in a position to endanger life, either the firer's or someone else's.

They were hauling things out of the hole now: bin-liner-wrapped shapes.

'I'll take McElwaine,' Boyd whispered to Haymaker. He felt a slight tap from the trooper's boot in agreement.

There. It looked like a Heckler & Koch G3: a good weapon. McElwaine was cradling the rifle like a new toy, discarding the bin-liner it had been wrapped in.

Boyd tightened his fist, and the M16 exploded into life. A hot cartridge-case struck his left cheek as Haymaker opened up also, but he hardly felt it. They were both firing bursts of automatic, the heavy, sickly smell of cordite hanging in the air about their heads.

McElwaine was thrown backwards, the G3 flying from his hands. Boyd saw the parka being shredded, dark pieces of flesh and bone spraying out from the massive exit wounds. Then McElwaine was on the ground, moving feebly. Boyd heard the 'dead man's click' from his weapon and changed magazines swiftly, then opened up again. McElwaine's body jumped and jerked as the 5.56mm rounds tore in and out of it.

He was aware that Conlan was down too. Haymaker changed mags also, then continued to fire. When they had emptied two mags each Boyd called a halt. They replenished their weapons and then lay breathing fast, their ears ringing and the adrenalin pumping through their veins like high-octane fuel. Haymaker was struggling not to laugh.

Boyd pressed the 'squash' button on the Landmaster radio to tell Taff and Raymond the mission had been a success. Then he and Haymaker lay motionless, rifles still in the shoulder, looking out on the meadow with its two shattered corpses.

Ten minutes they lay there, not moving – just watching. Then Boyd nudged Haymaker and the big man took off towards the bodies. Boyd pressed the squash button again, twice. Taff and Raymond would close in now.

Haymaker examined both bodies, then waved. Boyd grinned, then thumbed the switch on the radio once more.

'Zero, this is Mike One Alpha, message, over.'

'Mike One Alpha, send over.'

'Mike One Alpha, Ampleforth, over.'

'Zero, roger out.'

Boyd had given the code for a successful operation. In a few minutes a helicopter would arrive to spirit the SAS team away. The Green Army and the police would arrive to wrap up the more mundane details. Boyd ran over to Haymaker. The big trooper was kneeling by the bodies. It was hard to see the expression on his camouflaged face in the gathering twilight.

'Fucking weapons weren't loaded, boss. The magazines are still in the hole.'

Boyd shrugged, slipping on a pair of black Northern Ireland-issue gloves.

'That's not a problem.'

He reached into the hole and fetched the loaded magazines that the IRA men had not had time to fix to their weapons. Then he carefully loaded the G3 and an Armalite that was still in the cache, and placed them beside the two bodies.

'That's more fucking like it. No one will whinge about civil liberties now.'

The two men laughed. The adrenalin was still making them feel a little drunk. They turned at a noise and found Taff and Raymond approaching, grins all over their filthy faces.

'Scratch two more of the bad guys, eh boss?' Taff said.

'Damn straight.' Boyd lifted his head. He could hear the thump of the chopper off in the rain-filled sky. They had timed it nicely – there was just enough light for a pick-up.

'Right, let's clean up this place. I don't want any kit left lying around for the RUC to sniff over.' He paused. 'Well done, lads. This was a good one.'

'Bit of a payback for those poor bastards in Armagh,' Haymaker said. He nudged one of the broken bodies with his foot.

'You're playing with the big boys now, Paddy.'

3

Armagh

It was good to be out of the city, Early thought. Belfast was a depressing hole at times, as claustrophobic and as deadly as some Stone Age village in a jungle. There were all the little invisible boundaries. One street was safe, the one next to it was not. This was Loyalist, that was Republican. This was a safe pub, that was a death-trap. So much depended on names and nuances, even the way the people spoke, the things they said, the football teams they supported, the sports they played.

Not that Armagh was any different. He must remember that. But it was good to see green fields, cows grazing, tractors meandering along the quiet roads. Hard to believe these places were battlefields in a vicious little war.

He took the bus from Armagh city, through Keady and Newtownhamilton, down to Crossmaglen – 'Cross' to soldiers and locals alike. Early preferred travelling by bus. It was less risky than using a car, and fitted in with his identity as an unemployed bricklayer.

The bus was stopped at vehicle checkpoints three times in its journey south, and soldiers who seemed both tense and bored got on to walk up and down the aisle, looking at faces and luggage, and occasionally asking for ID. At two of the VCPs Early was asked his name, destination and the purpose of his journey. It amused and relieved him that the soldiers seemed to find him a suspicious-looking character. The other passengers stared stonily ahead when the bus was checked, but when the soldiers had left one or two of them smiled at him, commiserating. Early shrugged back at them, smiling in return. His false ID, his accent and his motives for travelling to Crossmaglen were impeccable. He was Dominic McAteer, a bricklayer looking for work with Lavery's Construction in the town.

Lavery's offices were in a small estate called Rathkeelan, to the north-west of Crossmaglen. Early got off the bus and stood looking around, hands in pockets, his duffle bag on his back. He bore no ID, but strapped to the inside of his right ankle was a compact Walther 9mm semiautomatic; not as effective as the Browning High Powers the SAS usually carried, but far more easily concealed. It could fit in his underpants if it had to.

Early passed beautifully painted murals on the whitewashed walls of the houses, the silhouettes of Balaclava-clad men bearing Armalites, and on one wall the recently repainted tally 'Provos 9 Brits 0' and below it the slogan 'One Shot, One Kill'.

His jaw tightened with anger for a second. His brother was one of those included in that score.

Then he recollected himself, and headed for the door of the nearest bar, whistling 'The Wild Colonial Boy'.

It was dark inside, as all Irish pubs were. He dumped his duffle bag with a sigh and rubbed the back of his thick neck. A cluster of men sitting and standing with pints in their hands paused in their conversation to look at him. He smiled and nodded. The barman approached, a large, florid man wiping a glass.

'What can I get you?'

'Ach, give us a Guinness and a wee Bush.'

The barman nodded. The conversations resumed. *Good Evening Ulster* had just started on the dusty TV that perched on a shelf near the ceiling. Early pretended to watch it, while discreetly clocking the faces of the other customers. No players present. He was glad.

The Guinness was good, as it always was nearer the border. Early drank it gratefully, and raised his glass to the barman.

'That's as good as the stuff in O'Connell Street.'

The barman smiled. 'It's all in the way it's kept.'

'Aye, but there's some pubs that don't know Guinness from dishwater. It's the head – should be thick as cream.'

'It's the pouring too,' the barman said.

'Aye. Ever get a pint across the water? They throw it out in five seconds flat and the head's full of bloody bubbles.'

The barman looked at him and then asked casually: 'You've been across the water, then?'

'Aye. But there's no work there now. I hear Lavery's has a job out here in Cross and needs some labourers. I'm a brickie meself, and sure there's bugger-all up in Belfast.'

'Ach, sure the city is gone to the dogs these days.'

'You're right.' Early raised his glass of Bushmills. '*Slainte*,' he said. He thought the barman relaxed a little.

'So you're down here for the work? This isn't your part of the world, then.' Early thought the other customers pricked up their ears at the barman's question. He was being cased. He doubted if any of these men were Provisionals, but they no doubt knew people who were, and in a small village like Crossmaglen, every outsider was both a novelty and a subject for scrutiny.

'Aye, I'm from Ballymena meself, up in Antrim.'

'Paisley's country.'

Early laughed. 'That big cunt. Oh aye, he's my MP. How's that for a joke?' Again, the slight relaxation of tension.

'If you're looking for work, you've come to the right place,' the barman said. 'The army never stops building in this neck of the woods. Their bases are as big as the town is. They're crying out for builders.'

Early scowled. 'I wouldn't fucking work for them if they paid me in sovereigns. No offence.'

The barman grinned.

'Would there be a B & B in the town? I need a place to stay – if these Lavery people take me on.'

The barman seemed to have relaxed completely, and was all bonhomie now. 'This is your lucky day. I've a couple of rooms upstairs I rent out in the summer.'

'Ah, right. What's the damage?'

'Fiver a night.'

Early thought, frowning. He had to appear short of cash. 'That's handy, living above a pub. Wee bit pricey though. How about knocking it down a bit, since I'd be here for a while, like. It's not like I'm some tourist, here today and gone tomorrow.'

'You get this job, and then we'll talk about it.'

'That'll do. I'm Dominic by the way.'

'McGlinchy?'

Early laughed. Dominic McGlinchy was the most wanted man in Ireland.

'McAteer.'

'Brendan Lavery,' the barman said, extending his hand. 'It's my brother you'll be working for.'

* * *

Early, blessing his luck, had been about to walk out to Rathkeelan to see about the job, but Brendan wouldn't hear of it. His brother, Eoin, would be in that night, he said. There was no problem about the job. Dominic could look the room over and have a bite to eat. Maggie, their younger sister, would be home from work in a minute, and she'd throw something together for them.

The room was small and simple but well kept, with a narrow bed, wardrobe, chair, dresser and little table. Through the single window Early could see the narrow back alleyways and tiny gardens at the rear of the street, and rising above the roofs of the farther buildings, the watch-towers of the security base with their anti-missile netting and cameras and infrared lights. He shook his head. It was hard to believe sometimes.

The door to the room had no lock, which was not surprising in this part of the world. Ulster had little crime worth speaking of that was not connected to terrorism, and this was, after all, Lavery's home he was staying in, not a hotel.

At the end of the long landing was the bathroom. Early ran his eyes over as much of the upstairs as he could, noting possible approach routes and escape routes. It had become second nature to him to view each place he stayed in as both a fortress and a trap. Satisfied, he went back downstairs.

The pub was filling up. Brendan Lavery was deep in conversation with a group of men at one end of the bar. Early immediately clocked two of them: Dermot McLaughlin and Eugene Finn, both players, and almost certainly members of the Provisional IRA's South Armagh brigade. Finn was an important figure. He had been a 'blanket man' in the Maze in the late seventies, before the Republican hunger strike that had resulted in eleven prisoners starving themselves to death. The Intelligence Corps believed that Finn might be the South Armagh Brigade Commander. McLaughlin was almost certainly the Brigade Quartermaster, in charge of weapons and explosives.

There was a woman at the bar: quite striking, dark-haired and green-eyed – a real Irish colleen. She seemed to be selling newspapers. When she saw Early she immediately approached him.

'*An Phoblacht?*'

'Eh? Oh aye, sure.' He bought an edition of the IRA newspaper and she smiled warmly.

'Brendan says you'll be staying with us for a while.'

'Aye, looks that way, as long as the work appears.'

'It will. I'll have the dinner ready in an hour. Why don't you have a chat with the boys?'

'You're Maggie, right?'

'That's right. And you're Dominic, from Ballymena. We don't get many Antrim men down here.'

'Maybe it's the climate.'

'Or the Brits.' She laughed teasingly. She was disturbingly attractive, Early thought. He did not like that. He did not want any distractions.

'You know, I haven't bought this for ten years,' he said lightly, holding up the paper. 'I've been across the water, building and digging all the way from London to Glasgow.'

'Ach, I thought maybe there was something in your accent.'

Early's blood ran cold, but he smiled at her and said: 'You pick these things up. Now I'm home I'll get rid of it. It's nice not to have some bastard calling you "Paddy" all the time. If there's one thing gets up my nose, it's that. Bloody English never stop to think we've names of our own.'

'You're right there – sure, they haven't a clue. It's a roast for tea, and spuds and cauliflower. That suit you?'

'Depends on how it's cooked.'

She laughed. 'Ach, don't you worry about that, Dominic. I'll keep the flesh on you.' Then she left, exiting via the door behind the bar.

Early wondered if he had been wise with his remarks about England. He didn't want to lay it on too thick.

He leaned on the bar.

'How about a pint there, Brendan? And sure, have one yourself. I have to keep me landlord sweet,' he called.

The barman laughed but Finn and McLaughlin did not. They were appraising Early frankly. He buried his face in *An Phoblacht*. Two 'volunteers' had been killed on active service in Tyrone. The SAS were suspected. It was, the paper said, a typical SAS assassination. The men had been unarmed; the weapons they had been found with planted on them after death.

'Bastards,' Early said softly, shaking his head.

'Aye, those fuckers get away with murder,' said a voice at this elbow.

It was Finn, standing beside him.

Early remained sorrowful and angry. 'It never stops, does it. Young boys dying in ditches. Will they ever leave us alone?'

Brendan Lavery set the brimming Guinness on the bar. 'Ach, sure, we're a good training ground for them. They don't give a damn. We're a nation of murderers to them.'

'Ireland unfree shall never be at peace,' Finn quoted, and drank from his own glass. Then he addressed Early again.

'You and me's going to be working together, Dominic.'

Early started. 'What?'

'Eoin – Brendan's brother – he's hit the big time, hasn't he, Brendan? He's taking on the world and his wife at the minute to build these bungalows they've contracted him for. Hiring all round him he is, like some Yank executive. Mind you' – Finn laid a finger against his nose – 'it's all on the QT. Most of the men working for him will be doing the double.' He meant that they were also on the dole. Finn and Lavery laughed together, and Early forced himself to smile.

'If it comes to that, the taxman doesn't know *I* exist, either.'

'That's the way it's meant to be, Dominic. Take all you can off the bastards, and give nothing back. So how did a Ballymena man hear about a job in Cross?'

'Ach, a man in the Crown in Belfast told me,' Early said, quite truthfully.

Finn nodded. 'A black hole, Ballymena. You'd not get a job up there, if you're the wrong colour.'

'Bloody right,' Early agreed sincerely. North Antrim was a Unionist stronghold in the same way South Armagh was Republican. He sipped at his Guinness, realizing he was being cased again.

'But it's different down here. There's always a welcome here for the right sort of man. Isn't that right, Brendan?'

The barman's reply was lost in the growing hubbub. The evening crowd was gathering and the TV was blaring at what seemed like full volume. Early would have liked to scan the crowd for familiar faces, as he had studied the mugshots of all the South Armagh players before travelling down. But he did not dare with Finn standing next to him.

Finn was a tall, slim man, grey-haired but fit-looking. He had a narrow, ruddy face with deep-set eyes that seldom smiled, even if the mouth did. He was responsible for a spate of sectarian murders in the late seventies, but all that had been pinned on him in court was possession of arms and IRA membership. He had once been quartermaster of the Armagh bunch, but had been promoted on his release from the Maze. An experienced man, he had many years' practice in killing, extortion and gunrunning. He knew who the Border Fox was, without a doubt, but it was unlikely that the sniper was Finn himself. He had graduated into a leader, a planner. He was a survivor from the early days of the Troubles, and hence the object of much respect in the Republican community.

Early would have liked to take him out behind the pub and put a bullet in the back of his fucking head, but instead he offered him a drink.

'Na, thanks, Dominic. I'll take ye up on it some other time, but tonight I have to keep me wits about me.'

Was there an op on tonight? Early wondered.

Finn leaned close. 'You're new here. Let me give ye a wee bit of advice. Don't let the bastards provoke you, or you'll get hauled in the back of a pig. They're pissed off at the minute because things have been a wee bit hot for them down here, but believe me, that's just the beginning. Now just keep your cool.' Finn looked at his watch, and then winked at Early.

The door of the pub burst open, startling those sitting next to it. A glass crashed to the floor in an explosion of beer. Men got to their feet cursing.

British soldiers were shouldering in through the door. They were in full combat uniform, with helmets and flak-jackets and cammed-up faces. An English voice shouted: 'Don't you fucking move!'

Eight soldiers, a full section, were in the pub now. Lights from vehicles outside were illuminating the front of the building. The crowd had gone silent.

'Turn off that fucking TV!' the English voice yelled, and Brendan pressed a button on the remote control, muting the volume.

'What the fuck?' Early said, genuinely surprised. Finn gripped his arms tightly. 'Don't move. The fuckers are just trying to annoy us.'

While four soldiers remained by the door, rifles in the shoulder, two pairs were walking through the pub, looking at faces. One of them kicked a chair over, receiving murderous looks, but no one said a word.

A soldier stopped in front of Finn and Early. He had a corporal's stripes on his arm.

'Hello, Eugene, me old mucker,' he said brightly. 'How's things, then?'

Finn looked him in the eye. 'I'm fine, thanks, Brit.'

The corporal grinned, his teeth bright in his darkly camouflaged face. 'Who's your friend? Any ID, mate?'

He was addressing Early. The SAS man tensed, then said clearly: 'Fuck off, you Brit bastard. Why can't you leave us alone?'

The soldier's grin vanished.

'That's not very polite, Paddy.'

'My name's not Paddy.'

'Give me some ID now, you fucking mick,' the corporal snarled.

Early produced his fake ID, a driver's licence issued in Coleraine. The corporal looked it over, then stared closely at him.

'You're a long way from home, Paddy.'

'So I've been told.'

The soldier nodded at Finn. 'I'd keep better company if I were you.'

'I'll keep the company I fucking well choose to. This is my country, not yours.'

'Have it your own way, arsehole. Outside now – and you too, Eugene. We don't want your friend getting lonely.'

Finn looked weary. 'Why don't you just drop it?'

The corporal gestured with the muzzle of his SA-80. 'Fucking outside – *now*. You can get there on your own two feet or you can be carried out – it's your choice.'

For once, Early was unsure what his reaction should be. He hesitated, but Finn gripped his arm again.

'Let's get it over with. Sure, all this wee shite wants it to put the boot in, and there's no point in wrecking Brendan's bar.'

'Don't you worry about my bar, Eugene,' Brendan called out. 'I'll claim the fucking lot back in compensation.'

But Finn and Early trooped out unresisting into the night. Army vehicles were parked there, their headlights blindingly bright. A hand shoved Early in the small of his back.

'In the fucking wagon, mick.'

Someone tripped him and his palms went down on the tarmac. A boot collided with his backside, sending him sprawling again. He felt the first stirrings of real anger. These pricks would certainly win no hearts and minds in this town.

He was pushed and shoved into the dark interior of an armoured Landrover. He heard Finn shouting, the sound of blows, and was dimly aware that people were pouring out of the pub into the square. There was a ragged surf of shouting, the beginnings of a mob. Then the metal door of the Landrover was clanged shut behind him.

A light flicked on. Sitting in the vehicle grinning at him was Cordwain.

4

'Well well, John,' Cordwain said. 'We meet again.'

They were not alone in the back of the Landrover. A third man sat there on one of the narrow seats in an SAS-pattern combat smock. He looked young, pink-cheeked, and he stared at Early with obvious fascination.

Cordwain, as always, was breezy and confident. He helped Early off the floor. Outside there was the sound of people screaming and yelling. Stones rebounded off the armoured sides of the vehicle and it swayed at bodies pushed against it. Cordwain tapped the partition that divided the driver's section from the back, for all the world like a millionaire signalling to his chauffeur. The engine roared into life and the vehicle began reversing.

'Sounds as though we've stirred up a bit of trouble,' Cordwain said. 'But that's all for the best.'

'Who are this lot?' Early asked. 'Greenjackets?'

'Yes. They've been here for four months, and they've lost four men.'

'Well, they're fucking heavy-handed.'

'They were meant to be. I'm trying to give you a bit of street cred in the Republican community. Also, we need to talk.'

Early looked at the third occupant of the Landrover. The vehicle was lurching, starting and stopping. The shouting outside continued.

'Who is this, then?'

'Lieutenant Charles Boyd, Ulster Troop,' the young man said. He had a public-school accent and didn't look old enough to grow a beard, but his eyes were cold and eager. They reminded Early of Eugene Finn's. There was no humour in them.

'So you're my back-up,' Early said. 'Hooray.'

Boyd frowned but Cordwain cut short any riposte.

'Charles here is one of the best young officers we've got,' he said. 'You may have heard of the incident in Tyrone a few days ago. Textbook stuff. Now you and he are going to do the same thing to the South Armagh Brigade.'

'The Armagh lot is a different kettle of fish. Since that fiasco at Loughgall in '87 they're tighter-knit than ever.'

'Oh, we know. But you seem to have started out on the right foot, becoming buddies with the biggest player in the area. My congratulations, John. You've been here less than a day and already you're rubbing shoulders with the head honcho.'

'Let's cut the crap, James. I can't sit in here in the middle of a riot all night. Give me the gen.'

'All right. The situation is as follows. I have most of the Group in Bessbrook at the moment, and 14 Company's people have covert OPs going in tonight. The riot is their cover. We'll search a few houses, insert the teams in the confusion – the usual thing.'

'How did you know I'd be in the bar?' Early interrupted.

'Hell, John, you should know better than that. You've been tailed ever since you got on the bus in Armagh.'

Early felt slightly annoyed with himself, for he had not noticed.

'We'll have the bar, Finn's house and McLaughlin's house all covered. Charles's boys will be looking after you. We'll use the old dead letterbox system for messages. Out beyond the centre beyond the town. You go out on the Castleblaney road, past the sports ground, and there will be an old milk churn in the ditch on the left-hand side. We site vehicle checkpoints there all the time. Leave your first comms there. We'll get word to you where the second will be. You should be able to go for a walk now and again – it's only a ten-minute stroll. In a place this small, we can't have the stuff that works in Belfast. Do you want a panic button installed? We could get it in your room tonight.'

Early shook his head. 'I want you to keep your distance as much as possible. These guys are nervous as cats already.'

'Have it your way, then. We've fibre optics, laser microphones, the whole heap, but you've got bugger-all but your wits and that peashooter you carry.'

'Suits me. Now I think it's time I was on my way, don't you?'

Cordwain listened to the commotion outside. It showed no signs of abating. 'Yes. There is one more thing though: we have to make it all look convincing. Nothing personal, John.'

Early cursed. 'Get on with it, then.'

Boyd punched him on the eye once, twice, three times. Early remained still, though the third punch produced a stifled groan from his lips.

'Lie down on the floor,' Boyd said in that plummy accent of his.

Early did so, and Boyd went to work on him with his boots. After a particularly savage kick in the ribs, Early vomited helplessly. Boyd grimaced. He was out of breath.

'Sorry, old chap. Got a bit carried away.'

Early spat out blood. 'I'll bet you did. Now throw me the fuck out of here.'

The rear door of the Landrover swung open and Early was pitched out head first. He hit the tarmac of the square heavily, coloured lights dancing brightly in his head, and for a moment could do nothing but lie there in the reek of the vehicle's exhaust fumes. There were feet around him. The tarmac was covered with fragments of glass and broken stone, and the sound of the crowd yelling seemed to hurt his very brain.

Strong hands grabbed him and hauled him away from the Landrover.

'Look what the fuckers did to him! The rotten bastards! Sure, he's never hurt a fly – only got here this afternoon.'

Early looked up painfully. It was Brendan Lavery, and beside him, Maggie. Her eyes were full of concern.

'Jesus, my head hurts.'

'They've split your head. Here, hold that hanky there. We'll get you inside. They did the same to Eugene. What a fucking wonderful country!'

He was dragged back to the bar, through a milling crowd of shouting people. The riot was impromptu, not staged like so many were, but it seemed no less vicious for all that. Soldiers were swinging batons, and Early heard the hollow boom of a plastic bullet being fired. Then there was a flare and a hiss, and the crowd was scattering. They were using CS. It was a hell of a way to rig up a meeting. He suspected that Cordwain and Boyd enjoyed it – it was just their fucking style.

People were coming back inside now, coughing and spluttering. Several of the pub's windows had been smashed to smithereens. Early noted the thick, flesh-coloured cylinder of a plastic bullet rolling on the floor, but the noise from outside was lessening. The CS had done the trick. His own nose began to tingle and he realized that the gas was seeping into the pub. A last trio of figures staggered inside and then the doors were closed. People pulled the curtains across the shattered windows, coughing, eyes streaming.

'How's your head now? Jesus, Dominic, you're going to have a hell of a shiner in the morning.' Maggie was looking at Early solicitously. There was dirt on her cheek and her hair was all over the place.

'I hope the dinner's not burned,' Early said, which got a laugh from her.

Suddenly Finn was there too, squatting down beside Maggie. His face was a mass of rising bruises and his lip was split and still oozing. But he grinned at Early.

'Didn't I tell you not to provoke them now? And there we are – a babe in arms taken out by the big bad soldiers and given a wee kicking. That's life in Cross for you, McAteer. Still want to stay?'

'Those bastards aren't getting rid of me. I hope the fuckers get shot,' Early croaked. And thinking of Boyd, he almost meant it.

Finn had become very grave. He wiped his split lip. 'If wishes were horses, beggars would ride. Do you see now, Ballymena man, what we're up against down here? There's no law in Cross except what we make ourselves. Those thugs can't represent the law or the government. How can they? The law operates by the consent of the governed, and we withhold our consent. They're as good as criminals.'

'Now, Eugene, don't you start,' Maggie admonished him. 'The man's just after getting beaten up and you're talking to him about politics.'

Finn rose, smiling. The smile still did not reach his eyes.

'You and me will have a wee talk about this another time, Dominic, after you've seen Eoin Lavery and got yourself that job. It's a desperate shame when the Brits pull in a man like yourself and give him the once-over; a man who's never been part of anything no doubt, a man as innocent as the day is long. You take care now, and watch this wee girl. I think she has an eye for you.'

Maggie swatted Finn with the cloth, and he laughed. Then he touched his bruised face tentatively.

'Have they made a right mess of me then, Maggie?'

'No more of a mess then there was before,' she retorted.

'And here's me going to be playing the bodhran down in Kilmurry this week, with me face looking like a potato. I doubt none of the local lassies will be giving me so much as a look.'

'Ach, Eugene, sure you know they'll be round you like flies on a jampot, just as usual, especially when you tell them how you got your bruises.'

He winked at her. 'You may be right there, wee girl. I must be going now. I've a feeling it's going to be a busy night. You look after Dominic now. The poor man looks a bit pale.'

Finn left them and went over to the door of the bar. He looked out, and signalled to two other men in the pub. One of them was McLaughlin. The trio exited silently.

Maggie was blushing, Early realized. But he noted it with only one portion of his mind. The rest was taken up with Finn's words. Had they been an echo of suspicion? It was too hard to say. And that reference to Kilmurry – it was in the Republic, and Cordwain would want to know about that. He would have to get a message through via the dead letterbox. He groaned. His body felt like one massive bruise. That bastard Boyd had enjoyed it, the smooth-chinned little shite.

'Let me help you up to your room,' Maggie said, helping him to his feet. 'I'll bring you up your tea later – there's a world of clearing up to do here. Never you worry about anything Eugene says. He's a passionate man, so he is, but he has reason to be.'

'I don't think he likes me,' Early said.

'Ach, that's just his way. He was born suspicious. What you need now is a bite to eat and then some sleep. It's bound to have been a long day.'

When he was finally alone in his room, Early found that someone had been through his things, discreetly, but not discreetly enough. He half hoped that it wasn't Maggie. He liked her, he realized. Not only that, she might be a way in. She seemed to know a lot about what was going on in the town, and her bed was as good a place to pump her for information as any. Early grinned to himself at the image that thought conjured up.

Just so long as Finn had been convinced by the evening's little charade. Early disliked the flamboyance of men like Cordwain and Boyd. He instinctively felt that it was counter-productive, fuelling the current enmity between soldiers and locals in the town. It certainly did not make his own job any easier.

His head and ribs throbbed. His eye was closing over rapidly. The 'kicking' had been convincing enough, anyway.

He padded out of his room and down the hallway to the bathroom, to wet a towel for his eye. The light was on inside and the door was ajar. He peeked round the doorway carefully. Maggie was in there, her back to him as she leaned out the window. She was wearing a short bathrobe and he had a wonderful view of her long, pale legs, a glimpse of her round buttocks. She was talking to someone outside, and leaned out until Early thought she would flip over the sill and out the window. Despite the splendid sight before him, Early tried to listen in on her conversation, but could make out little. He ducked back hurriedly as she backed in from the window carrying something in her hands, something long and heavy wrapped in plastic.

Early tiptoed back along the landing, cursing silently. She had been holding an AK47.

There was uproar in Crossmaglen that night. The streets were full of the roar of engines. Saracen armoured cars and Landrovers, police 'Hotspurs' and 'Simbas' went to and fro disgorging troops and heavily armed RUC officers. Sledgehammers smashed down doors and soldiers piled into houses amid a chaos of cursing and shouting, breaking glass, screaming children. Households were reduced to shambles as the Security Forces searched house after house, the male occupants spread-eagled against the sides of the vehicles outside, the females shrieking abuse.

Carpets were lifted up, the backs of televisions wrenched off, the contents of dressers and wardrobes scattered and trampled. In the confusion, a covert surveillance team from the Group were inserted into the disused loft of a house in the heart of the town and set up an OP, peering out at the world from gaps in the roof tiles or minute holes in the brickwork. Finally, their work done, the army and police withdrew, leaving behind them a trail of domestic wreckage and huddles of people staring at the chaos of their homes. It had all gone like clockwork. From their concealed position up above, the SAS team watched silently the comings and goings of the town.

5

Bessbrook

'At last, we have intelligence,' Cordwain said, with an almost visible glow of satisfaction.

Lieutenant Boyd raised an eyebrow. 'Our man has turned something up already, has he?'

'Yes and no.' The roar of a Wessex helicopter landing on the helipad outside rendered conversation impossible for a moment. Bessbrook had one of the busiest heliports in Europe. There were Lynxes, fragile little Gazelles, sturdy troop-carrying Pumas, and the old Wessexes, the workhorse of the British Army. The base itself was surrounded by a four-metre-high fence, topped with anti-missile netting and bristling with watchtowers and sangars. In the Motor Transport yard were a motley collection of Saracens, hard-roofed four-ton trucks, Landrovers and Q cars. Bessbrook was a mix of high-tech fortress, busy bus station and airport. In truth, it was also something of a slum for the assorted British Forces personnel who had to live within its cramped confines in the ubiquitous Portakabins, reinforced with concrete and sandbags against mortar attack.

'No,' Cordwain went on when he could hear himself speak. 'You may find it hard to believe, but the initial info comes from across the border, from the Special Branch section of the Gardai.'

Boyd was incredulous. 'The micks have turned something up, and they're handing it to us?'

'They're afraid, Charles. They think they may have stumbled across something big and they want us to pull their potatoes out of the fire for them.'

Cordwain turned to the wall of his office, on which was pinned a large, garishly coloured map of South Armagh. He tapped the map.

'I Corps has been given information by them of an Irish music festival which is to be held in the hamlet of Kilmurry, County Louth, in two days' time. Kilmurry is approximately one kilometre from the River Fane, which, as you know, marks the border between north and south in that part of the world. An ideal jumping-off point for any operation. This morning our man Early in Cross utilized the DLB and left a message informing us that Eugene Finn will be at that festival. The Gardai have also informed us that they have identified at least eight major players from Louth or Monaghan ASUs heading north towards the border. Their routes all converge on Kilmurry.'

'A regular PIRA convention,' Boyd said. 'Have we anything else?'

'No. But I believe that this is not just a confab, Charles. We've hit Cross pretty hard in the past few days. It's my belief the Provos are going to stage some kind of spectacular, and Kilmurry will be their base of operations. This bash is their cover.'

'And because this place is in the Republic, there's not a damned thing we can do about it,' Boyd said bitterly.

'Just so. I cannot authorize an incursion into the Irish Republic, Charles, and there is no time to refer it to the CLF or to the Secretary of State. Our hands are tied.'

'So what can we do?' Boyd asked.

'Like you, I would dearly love to launch a preemptive strike, but the risk of adverse publicity is too high. There will be hordes of people in Kilmurry once this festival gets under way. There is no question of moving in there – the Provos have planned that part of it well. But I believe they will move north once they have been fully prepped, to launch a strike somewhere in the vicinity of Cross. That we *can* do something about. Look at the map.'

Boyd joined his superior at the wall and together they stared at the complex pattern of small roads and hills, villages and hamlets, rivers and bogs.

'See here, this dismantled railway, that more or less follows the line of the Fane?'

Boyd nodded, and Cordwain went on.

'There are old cuttings all along its length, ideal places to conceal a group of men and form them up for a riving crossing. The Fane is broad, so they'll need a boat. It'll be a night operation of course. I think they'll get themselves ferried across where the cuttings, the river and the border all meet. Here.' Cordwain's finger stabbed at a point on the map.

'Now look north, only half a kilometre. There's a hill here, with an old ring-fort on top. Drumboy Fort, it's called; we've had OPs on it in the past. There is your ideal spot to wait and intercept them. Good fields of fire in all directions, no civvy houses close by, and a perfect view of the river, and thus the border.'

'You don't expect them to be picked up by car, then?' Boyd asked. Cordwain shook his head.

'The nearest road is half a kilometre away. They'll have to move across country to get to it. And we have all the roads down there sewn up tighter than a nun's knickers. No, my belief is that they'll yomp it, move across country to some prearranged RV and then perhaps meet up with a few friends north of the border before moving in on their objective.'

'Which will be?'

Cordwain shrugged. 'I have no idea, though I have my suspicions. If you extend a line from the Fane up past Drumboy Fort, where does it take you?'

Boyd peered at the map, then burst out: 'The base! Crossmaglen security base! But that can't be right.'

'That's what I thought. It would be foolhardy, to say the least. But you'll have to bear in mind, Charles, that these jokers are after something big. Not a mortar – they'll be travelling too light for that. But an ambush, certainly, perhaps of a foot patrol. I think they intend to wipe out an entire patrol, engage it face to face and then blow it away.'

Boyd whistled softly. 'What about their strength?'

'This will be a big operation in their terms, comparable to Loughgall perhaps. I think you can bank on at least ten or twelve of them.'

They turned away from the map and resumed their seats. Another helicopter took off, loaded to the gills with men and equipment. It was a Greenjacket fire team being airlifted out on rural patrol.

'Fuck,' Boyd said clearly. 'This is all surmise though, isn't it? All we know for sure is that a bunch of players will be at a music festival close to the border.'

'Indeed, but I'll bet both our arses they aren't attending it to sit and fiddle. No, they'll be moving north – you can count on it.'

Boyd's eyes shone. If he pulled off a large-scale ambush on a sizeable PIRA force it would be an enormous coup for the Government, the army and the SAS. But also for Lieutenant Charles Boyd.

'I have four men tied up in the OP in Cross itself, but twelve men available here, a multiple of three bricks. That should do it.'

Cordwain was not so sure.

'I'd rather fly in some of the Special Projects team from G Squadron in Hereford.'

'But we haven't the time. And we don't have enough evidence to go on. We'll have egg all over our faces if we get G Squadron all the way over here and then nothing materializes.'

Cordwain paused, clearly uneasy. 'There is that, of course . . .'

'James, twelve SAS troopers will take out anything the Provos can throw at them.' Boyd appeared invincibly confident. Cordwain studied him for a moment. The young officer clearly still felt himself to be on a roll after the successful Tyrone operation, and wanted to add further lustre to his laurels. That was no bad thing, so long as it did not lead to overconfidence. But his brashness was appealing, and it was true that they had very little to go on. Cordwain did not put a lot of faith in Early's chances of infiltrating the South Armagh Brigade, but here on a platter was a chance to wipe them out wholesale; the ultimate 'clean kill'.

'All right,' he said at last. 'I'll make out the necessary orders. But what I'm giving you is a reactive OP, Charles. I'm not giving you licence to run amok through the countryside. I want you to keep that stretch of the Fane under observation and only to react under the most stringent circumstances. The last thing we need is twelve troopers staging a rerun of the OK corral in Armagh. And we will also liaise with Lieutenant Colonel Blair of the Greenjackets. His men will form your back-up – and Early's – until this op is over. Is that clear?'

'Perfectly. If you'll excuse me then, James, I'll go and give the boys a Warning Order. They'll be chuffed to fuck.'

Boyd left like a schoolboy let out for the holidays. Cordwain stared at the map thoughtfully for a long time. It was disquieting, to say the least, to be sanctioning an operation with so little intelligence to go on, but then intelligence was so thin on the ground in this part of the world. Not like Tyrone, or Belfast, where there were 'Freds', renegade Republicans, aplenty.

If this operation turned out as successfully as he hoped they might even be able to dispense with Early's services, and that would be another bonus. Early was a hot potato, with his MI5 handlers to be placated and his stubborn bloody-mindedness. Not a team player, but then undercover agents seldom were.

Cordwain shook his head as though a fly buzzed at it, trying to free himself of a sense of unease. He had the strangest feeling that Boyd did not quite know what he was up against, and he had an urge to cancel the whole operation, or at least scale it down. But it was on his plate alone. He could not involve the RUC, because they were not equipped to deal with a face-to-face confrontation with a heavily armed band of terrorists, nor with the covert surveillance that was needed to track them down. No, this was a job for the SAS alone, the sort of mission that they specialized in and relished.

Why then the uneasiness?

He bent over his desk, and began writing the orders that would take Boyd's command out into Bandit Country.

6

Kilmurry, County Louth

The bar was crowded with people, hot, noisy, hazy with tobacco smoke. In one corner a knot of musicians were playing a frantic, foot-tapping jig and most of the throng were clapping and stamping in time with the music. Pint glasses, empty and full, stood by the hundred on the bar and the tables or were clasped in sweaty hands.

In the upstairs room the hubbub below could be heard as a vague roar of sound echoing up through the floorboards. The long upper room had been booked in the name of Louth Gaelic Football Club. The irritating noise seeping up from the noisy bar below would nullify the effectiveness of any bugs planted in the place.

There were twenty-three men in the room, sitting round a long dining table or lounging against the walls. Heavy duffle bags littered the floor and on the table itself crouched two angular, blanket-draped shapes. The men were smoking rapidly, talking in low voices, chuckling or scowling as the mood took them. They comprised the bulk of two PIRA brigades. Some of them were elated at their numbers, some were nervous.

Eugene Finn entered the room rubbing his hands and smiling his cold smile.

'Don't worry, boys. The dickers are all in place and the landlord knows the form. This is a private room. The Gardai will need a warrant to enter it and we happen to know they don't have one.'

'Aye, but what about when we leave?' one of the men asked sourly.

'When we leave, Seamus, there's not a force in the whole of Ireland that'll be capable of stopping us.'

'It's bloody madness,' Seamus Lynagh, commander of the Monaghan Brigade, exclaimed. 'It might be all right for you boyos in the north, but the Gardai will tail us all the way to the border, and when we come back they'll slap the cuffs on us.'

'They won't be able to tail you,' Finn said firmly.

'What are you, Eugene – a fucking magician?'

Some of the men laughed. Eugene Finn grinned humourlessly. 'Maybe I am, Seamus, maybe I am. Or maybe I'm Santa Claus. I come bearing gifts.'

He leaned over the table and with a swift gesture whipped the blankets from the shrouded forms standing there. Everyone straightened, and one man gave a low whistle.

Lying supported on the table by their bipods were two American-made 7.62mm M60 machine-guns, their barrels gleaming in the dim light of the room.

'Jesus, Mary and Joseph,' Lynagh breathed. 'Where'd you get them?'

'Courtesy of the US National Guard,' Finn smirked. 'A trawler picked them up for us. Caught them in its nets, so it did.'

Lynagh was running his hands over one of the weapons as though it were the body of a woman.

'These fuckers chew through concrete like it's paper. They're as good as the GPMGs that the Brits use. Better, maybe.'

'Are you willing to listen to the plan now?' Finn asked.

'Aye, I'll listen, Eugene. I won't promise you a bloody thing though, not till I've heard it through.'

Finn produced a pair of rolled-up maps and began pinning them to one wall. All the men immediately recognized the familiar contours of the border. For them it was home turf, the countryside of their very backyards.

'Here we are, boys, our feet tapping to jigs in Kilmurry here. Now look up to the border. See the old railway . . .'

'Sure, I know that place well,' one man put in. 'It's all overgrown with brambles and stuff. You could hide an army in there.'

'Thanks, Sean,' Finn said icily, and the man looked away, red in the face.

'That is where we form up, boys, all twenty-four of us: two platoons of twelve men each. I will take one, and Seamus the other. Each platoon will have an M60. But we're not moving out all in a bunch – far too easy for the Brits to keep tabs on us that way. No, we'll split up once we're across the river, Seamus's men going to the west of Drumboy Fort, and my lot going to the east. We'll meet up again in Clonalig, and there'll be two transits waiting for us there, ready to take us to the objectives.'

A storm of voices broke out.

'How are we getting across the river?'

'Who'll have the M60s?'

'Who's meeting us in Clonalig?'

But the main question was voiced by Seamus Lynagh as he held up a hand for quiet.

'What the fuck are we going to hit, Eugene?' he asked softly.

48

Finn smiled coldly, and jabbed the map with a finger.

'That. Crossmaglen RUC station. We're going to wipe the peelers off the face of the earth.'

Another storm of noise. Lynagh shook his head angrily.

'You're fucking crazy, Finn. The army will be all over us in minutes.'

'No, Seamus. You see, while your platoon is taking out the RUC station – just like Ballygawley, lads, eh? – my platoon will be covering the approach roads, ready to take out any reinforcements the peelers call in.'

'You're fucking mad,' Lynagh said, amazed.

'Twelve men, armed to the teeth. We have medium machine-guns, RPGs, even a fucking two-inch mortar. We'll make sure that not so much as a mouse gets out of that base. And if a mobile patrol comes along, then we'll fucking destroy it. What do you say, Seamus? Are you ready to go to war?'

Men were clamouring, laughing in the room, their eyes shining. Lynagh looked troubled.

'All right, Eugene, we're in. But Christ help you if this turns out to be another Loughgall.'

'It won't, Seamus. We're about to hit the Brits harder than they've ever been hit in Ireland before.'

It was a bright, sunny morning. Early rolled out of bed, groaning at the pain of his bruises. Saturday morning. He had, thankfully, the weekend in front of him before he had to start work as a labourer at Lavery's building site. He had his job, now. In fact he seemed to be quickly becoming a member of the family. He smiled, remembering the sight of Maggie's long legs and taut buttocks in the bathroom, then frowned as he remembered what she had in her hands. They were all in it up to their necks, even the bloody women. Still, it meant that if he made any progress with her he would be furthering the cause of British intelligence as well as getting his end away. The thought made him grin again.

Automatically, he reached under the bed and checked the automatic and the spare mags, tucked into his shoe. A daft place to conceal a weapon, which is why no one ever looked there.

He wondered if the DLB had worked, if Cordwain had got the message about Finn. Early didn't like the system. It was old, prone to tampering, and somehow amateurish. But there was no chance they could use the 'live letterbox' here: a man in a Q car waiting to debrief and brief him at some prearranged spot. It was too risky. The whole bloody thing was too risky.

Maggie was cooking breakfast for her two brothers when Early came downstairs, yawning and scratching his head. There was a delicious smell of cooking bacon in the air.

'Jesus, Dominic, your face looks like a wee one's finger-painting,' Brendan said, pouring him a cup of tea.

'Feels like a bloody football, so it does,' Early said, touching his swollen eye gingerly. But then he turned to Eoin Lavery, his employer, who was munching on fried soda bread silently.

'Don't worry though. I'll be at work on Monday morning all right.'

Eoin waved a fork. 'Ach now, Dominic, Brendan here has been telling me what those bastards – excuse me, Maggie – did to you. There's no rush. We'll give it to Tuesday, and if you do a bit of overtime towards the end of the week, sure we'll say that makes up for it.'

'Thanks, Eoin,' Early said. Maggie set a heavily laden plate in front of him, smiling. 'There, get that down you, Dominic.' She was wearing a floral-print dress that seemed to emphasize the curves of her figure. Early's fork paused halfway to his mouth as he watched her walk back towards the kitchen, the morning light catching the reddish glints in her hair. When he remembered to eat again he found both the Lavery brothers grinning at him like clowns.

He lingered after breakfast, rehearsing in his mind the route to the second DLB point, speculating on what Finn was up to across the border, and thinking about how satisfying it would be to feel his fist impacting with Boyd's nose. Then he started as he realized that Maggie was talking to him.

'What? Sorry, I was a thousand miles away, so I was.'

'That's all right, Dominic. I was aking you if you'd like to go for a wee walk this afternoon. It's such a lovely day.'

'I'd love to, aye,' he said, and found that he meant it.

It was warm, and the sun was high and bright in a blue sky. Very un-Irish weather, Early thought, and almost said so to the girl walking beside him until he realized how odd it would sound, and cursed himself for his lack of concentration. He was effectively behind enemy lines here, even though he could see the watch-towers of Cross Security Forces base less than a mile away, and could make out a Lynx sinking down, distant as a dragonfly, bringing another brick back from rural patrol.

They sat down on the springy turf and Maggie opened the small bag she had brought with her. They were on a hillside to the south of Cross, and could look down to where the Fane meandered through the hills and faded into the distance. The Republic of Ireland lay on the far side of the river's sunlit bank. It was hard to believe in the savage little war which flickered to and fro over such beautiful country as this. It all looked too peaceful and quiet to harbour anything more sinister than the odd poacher.

Maggie produced a bottle of white wine, two glasses and a corkscrew. She asked Early to do the honours, and as he wrestled with the cork she produced a small pair of binoculars and began sweeping the land to the south with them.

'What are you looking for?' he asked her lightly, pouring the wine.

'Birds,' she said absently. 'You get some very odd birds about here at this time of year.'

'I'll bet.'

She lowered the binoculars and sipped her wine. 'Good stuff this, so it is. I hope Brendan won't miss it.'

'So you've brought me out birdwatching, then,' he said.

'Yes. I hope you don't mind, Dominic.'

'Ach, no.' He lay back in the grass and closed his eyes, letting the sun warm him, but despite his appearance his heart was beating fast. Maggie was checking the lie of the land south to the border and Kilmurry, where Finn was skulking. And what was more, she had the newcomer with her, so she could keep an eye on him. Early smiled to himself. She was a smart girl, killing two birds with one stone. He would have to get another message through to Cordwain, let him know that there might be something happening down along the Fane valley. Tonight perhaps.

The Lynx roared overhead, flattening the grass and billowing Maggie's hair out behind her. She watched its flight path intently, and nodded to herself, no doubt noting it down as routine. Early tried not to let his tension show. Here was his chance to find out what was going down. Clearly Finn's absence and Maggie's birdwatching were connected.

'Tell me about yourself,' he said. 'How come a pretty wee girl like you wasn't married off years ago?'

She looked at him. 'I was married.'

'What happened?'

Again, the practised sweep with the binoculars.

'He was shot by the Brits. They said he was in the IRA, and he was supposed to have been caught in some ambush. When he died I took back my old name. That was two years ago.'

'What was your married name then?'

'Kelly.'

Early thought fast. Two years ago one Patrick Kelly had died in the abortive attack on Loughgall RUC station, along with seven other Provisionals. It had been the SAS's biggest success in Northern Ireland, and had effectively wiped out the East Tyrone Brigade. Kelly, a hot-head, had been an IRA quartermaster. He had been shot down, rifle in hand, in the road outside Loughgall.

He opened his eyes. This woman was very probably at the heart of the South Armagh Brigade. She probably knew who the Border Fox was.

'I'm sorry,' he said.

She smiled down at him. 'That's all right. He was an eejit, was Patrick; a lovely man, but like a wee boy sometimes. He made me feel like his mother.'

She looked like a young schoolteacher, or a young mother, not like the hardened activist Early now knew her to be. He reached up a hand and brushed her cheek gently. She did not pull away.

'Did you never think of leaving?'

'Never. My family is here, my life is here. One day I'll be here still and they' – she tossed her head at the frowning watch-towers of the base – 'they'll be gone, and Ireland will be at peace at last.'

Early felt the beginnings of irritation at hearing the old platitudes come so easily from such a young mouth. If British 'occupation' ended, then everything would be hunky-dory.

Their minds all worked the same way. It was like hearing parrots mouth words they could not understand. But he did not let his irritation show. Instead he gently pulled her head towards him, and brushed her lips with his own. He felt an answering caress for a moment, then she pulled away. She was blushing, he realized, like some schoolgirl on a date.

'If ever you need any help, or anyone to turn to, Maggie, then I'd be happy if you thought of me,' he said softly.

She stared out over the lush green landscape that marked the border between two countries, a decades-old battlefield.

'Thanks, Dominic, but I hardly even know you.'

Then she took up the binoculars again, and began scanning the border as alertly and professionally as a soldier in an OP.

7

Drumboy Hill, South Armagh

Boyd stopped in the dark of the night and turned to Haymaker.

'What do you make that, then?'

'Four hundred, boss, give or take a metre.'

Boyd nodded. One more leg to go and they were at the final RV before the objective. Haymaker was pacer for the multiple, and was counting out the metres they logged on each bearing of the compass they navigated by.

Boyd looked at the tiny luminous arrows on the compass, lined them up, and found a reference point in that direction. It was not easy. It had clouded, and the night was as black as pitch. They were navigating by bearings and pacings alone, cross-checking when they came to a road or track, or a slope, which would be a huddle of brown contour lines on the tiny map. Most of the map Boyd had memorized, so as to avoid checking it during the 'tab', or Tactical Advance by Bounds. Once, however, he had had to get it out, throw a poncho over his head to hide the glow of the minuscule red penlight, and then continue on his way.

He was that most dangerous of phenomena found on a battlefield, an officer with a map. The thought would have made him grin had he been less knackered.

Every man in the twelve-strong multiple was weighed down with over one hundred pounds of equipment, weaponry and ammunition. They were supposed to range over the ground in three four-man fire teams, their arcs of fire supporting each other, but it was so dark that they were in single file, every man occasionally touching the bergen on the back of the man in front to check he was still in the file. Navigation-wise, the pitch-darkness was a pain in the arse, but it was a blessing also. It meant that, barring disasters, they would make it to the objective completely unobserved.

They set off again. Boyd was his own point man – something tactically unsound, which he personally did not like, but as he was navigating, there was no alternative. Farther back in the stumbling, sweating and quietly cursing file the sergeant, Gorbals McFee, was check-navigating to make sure the young officer did not go astray. Gorbals was a tiny Glaswegian who was nonetheless one of the most frightening men Boyd had ever known. Five foot six, with a shock of violently red hair and a temper to match, he had been in the SAS since before the Falklands, and when Boyd could decipher his accent, he found him to be a superb soldier and NCO.

The weaponry and equipment of the troopers were plentiful and varied. Boyd carried an Armalite AR15 rifle, as did most of the others. But there were two 7.62mm General Purpose Machine Guns in the team also, as well as three M79 grenade-launchers, which looked vaguely like huge, single-barrelled shotguns. In addition, each man had a 9mm Browning High Power pistol holstered at his thigh, for all the world, Boyd thought, like the Lone Ranger.

But that was what they were, he realized. The guys in white hats, the posse out to get the villains.

Every trooper carried, in addition to his own personal ammunition, a belt of two hundred rounds for the GPMGs, a pair of fragmentation and smoke grenades, and a claymore antipersonnel mine. A particularly ugly little weapon, the claymore was a shaped charge of P4 which would blow several hundred ball-bearings in the face of any attacker and could be set off manually or by a trip-wire. It was ideal for perimeter security, as the Americans had found in Vietnam.

Two men each carried in addition a 66mm Light Anti-tank Weapon. A recoilless shoulder-fired missile, the '66' was light and easy to use, and was a single-shot throw-away item. It was very rarely carried in Northern Ireland, but Boyd had brought along a couple in case the opposition had RPG7 rocket-launchers. He believed in fighting fire with fire.

Other men in the multiple were weighed down with a variety of night-surveillance equipment and two of them were carrying 'Classic', a motion detector which was to be buried in the ground to detect the vibration of approaching footsteps. All in all, Boyd thought, they were equipped to fight a minor war all on their own.

He did not know it, but that was exactly what they would have to do.

They reached the objective. There was a faint wind blowing and the cloud was clearing somewhat. It was becoming a little lighter. There might even be a moon later on, though Boyd hoped not.

The multiple shrugged off their bergens within the earth banks of the old ring-fort on Drumboy Hill, and went into all-round defence. Individual Weapon Sights were switched on, NVGs swung down over their eyes. The SAS troopers waited for any sign that they had been followed or otherwise compromised. Thirty minutes they lay there, unmoving, and then Gorbals McFee went round the hollow ring, tapping each man's boot with his own.

The men worked in pairs. As one remained alert and on guard, the other got out an entrenching tool and began digging. Still others left the fort to sight the claymores so that they would blow laterally across every approach to the perimeter, and one fire team under Haymaker took 'Classic' out with them to seed the approaches from the south with the buried sensors. He would bury the sensors, leaving only the tiny whip-antennae above ground, and would map their locations for later retrieval. Each of the sensors, Gorbals had been careful to explain to him, was worth £5000, and if he lost any it would be docked out of his pay.

Haymaker was not sure if the little Glaswegian had been joking or not, but he didn't intend to take any chances. He had squared greaseproof paper folded in his pocket to make a foot-by-foot grid of the area where the sensors were to be buried.

The men remaining within the banks of the earth fort dug shell scrapes and began camouflaging them with scrim nets and local vegetation. They would have to lie up in the fort for a day at least, waiting for the Provos to make their move, and they could not afford to be discovered by any of the locals.

No light was allowed, and no one spoke. The PRC 351 man-portable radio was set on whisper, but radio silence was to be maintained until contact. Boyd also had a 'SARBE', a surface-to-air rescue beacon, which was only to be used as a last resort, if the multiple needed to leave in a hurry. He could not imagine needing it.

The troopers were all wearing 'goon boots': rubber over-shoes that fitted their combat boots and left no distinctive army-boot tread-marks for the locals to find and examine later. But they made the feet uncomfortably hot. Conversely, the men's bodies were beginning to chill as the exertion of the night march wore off and the breeze hit the sweat that slicked their bodies and dampened their clothes. A few dug out thick Norwegian shirts from their bergens, but most were content to shiver and wait for the summer dawn, which was only a few hours off.

Haymaker made it back in, hands raised above his head so that the sentries would know who it was. The claymores were armed and the men retired to their camouflaged scrapes. Soon the old ring-fort was quiet as the men took turns at grabbing a few minutes' sleep. They were in position, ready for the show to begin.

8

Crossmaglen

Sunday morning. Early was at mass with the Laverys in St Patrick's, Cross's parish chapel. He was wearing a tie, something he hated, and Maggie was sitting beside him with her prayer-book in her lap and the sunshine was coming through the stained-glass windows setting her tawny hair aflame with colour and light. She was beautiful, Early thought, but also dangerous. And she had seemed tense all this morning, hardly speaking a word to him. He was sure that today, or tonight, Finn had something planned. He wondered if that gut feeling were worth a message via the DLB, and decided not.

He had hardly been out of Maggie's sight for a day and a half. Either she liked having him near her, or she was suspicious of him and was keeping him where she could keep an eye on him. Early did not like it. It had all been too easy, had happened too quickly, and his beating up at the hands of the 'Brits' could not completely explain her solicitude.

Suddenly he was glad of the often irritating weight of the pistol at his ankle.

The service went on and on. Early's mind wandered. He began thinking of Jeff, his younger brother, who had died in this very town, his head ripped off by a high-calibre bullet. There had been seven years between them, so they had never been as close as Early would have liked – sometimes more like uncle and nephew than anything else. Jeff would have tried for the SAS in time, and would have made it, Early thought. He had been more of a team player, who got along with everybody. Little Jeff, his brother, whose dying body the mobs had laughed over in Crossmaglen. Early wondered suddenly if Maggie had been there, jeering over the body with the rest. The thought made his face ugly with hatred, and he bowed his head so the priest might not see it.

Mass ended at last, and they trooped out into the July sunshine. Maggie took Early's arm.

'Come on, Dominic, I'll walk you home. The roast will take a wee while yet in the oven, so there's no hurry.'

They strolled arm in arm down the street towards the square. The kerbstones here were painted green, white and orange and Early could see the Irish tricolour flying from several flagpoles.

A four-man foot patrol passed them on both sides of the street, SA-80s held upwards in the 'Belfast Cradle'. The NCO gave Early's face a quick look, then moved on. Had Early been identified as a player, the soldier would have engaged him in conversation. It was both a subtle form of harassment and intelligence-gathering at its most basic level.

Maggie looked through the soldiers as though they didn't exist.

'Tell me about yourself, Dominic. You're a Ballymena Catholic, which is rare enough. Your family's still up in Antrim, then?'

Early's mind clicked through all his bogus background. It had been carefully researched for him, and the fact that his roots truly did lie in the north of the Province helped him with his falsehoods.

'Ach, I was a late child, so I was, and an only one. Me ma and da are both dead this five years. After me ma went I left the place, decided to chance me arm across the water, you know – building like, and bar work. I was all over the place. But I came back. We never fitted in over there, not really. They always see you as a thick mick when it comes to the crunch. And I swore I'd never let another Brit call me "Paddy" as long as I lived. I suppose that's what got me this.' He touched his black eye.

Maggie squeezed his arm. 'Just right. We don't mix, Dominic, the Brits and us. Ach, they're not all bad, but once the English and Irish get together, there's always trouble. There's too much water under the bridge, too many years of oppression.'

Too much claptrap talked, Early thought, but he only nodded to her words.

'We're fighting a war here in the North, Dominic. Ireland needs all her sons.' Suddenly she stopped. In a moment her arms were around him and she was kissing him lightly on his lips. He felt her palms flat against his back and thanked his lucky stars that he had never worn a shoulder-holster.

'What was that for?' he asked her when she released him.

'For standing up for yourself in the bar that night. For not just being polite or careful. I think you have a stubborn streak in you, Dominic. I don't think you like to take things lying down.'

Early laughed. 'You may be right there.'

They walked on, and finally came back to the bar. Brendan was in the lounge, wiping tables. He nodded and grunted as they came in. The place was full of the smell of roasting meat, potatoes and rich gravy.

'Come upstairs,' Maggie said to Early, and led him by the hand.

They went into her room, an airy, cushion-covered place with a wide bed and pastel-coloured walls. Early began to sweat. She shut the door.

They sat on the bed and she took him by the hands again.

'Listen, Dominic, you said that I could turn to you for help any time I needed it.'

'I did. And you said you hardly knew me, which is true.' His voice sounded hoarse. He was trying to discreetly note any other way out, wondering what kind of field of fire the window would give. The gun strapped to his ankle suddenly seemed huge, obtrusive.

'Aye, I did. But I have a feeling about you, Dominic. We need people like you. Men who aren't afraid to stand up for themselves, who have common sense, who share our views.'

'Who's we?' Early asked. Her hand loosened his tie and begun unbuttoning his shirt.

'I think you know, Dominic. The Volunteers. The men who are fighting to make Ireland free.'

She drew close. Her hand slipped inside his shirt and was caressing his chest. She kissed his neck. There was something clinical, determined about her that made Early tense.

She was looking for a concealed weapon.

'Shiner or no, you're a lovely-looking man, you know that? You're all muscle.'

'It's the work,' he said lamely. He was torn between lust and fear. Her perfume rose in his nostrils. He kissed her lips, her ear, but was frantically trying to figure out how he could keep the ankle-holster concealed.

'You're just out of mass,' he said. 'Funny time to be doing a thing like this.'

Her hand had found his penis, and was carressing it gently. He could not help but respond.

'Oh, I know. It's a great sin, isn't it?'

'You'll let the roast burn in the oven, then?'

'To hell with the roast. What do you think, Dominic? Are you willing to help me? Are you willing to help your country?'

'Yes. Yes I am.'

She grinned at him, then bent her head and in a moment had taken his swollen member into her mouth. Early groaned as she worked on it, sucking and licking, her head moving up and down in his crotch. He buried his hands in her glorious hair, incredulous, but profoundly relieved.

Thank Christ, he thought. I managed to keep my trousers on.

Late that same Sunday, across the border, the room above the Kilmurry bar was humming with activity. Weapons, ammunition and other items of military equipment were scattered all over the floor. Men were oiling their rifles, loading magazines, or packing small rucksacks in preparation for the operation that night. In a quieter corner, Eugene Finn and Seamus Lynagh were going over the plan yet again.

'So this boat you have arranged will make two trips across the Fane, twelve men each time, and the drop-off points will be different,' Lynagh said.

'Aye,' Finn replied wearily. 'You'll be dropped off further to the west, about a mile south of Art Hamill's bridge. My ASUs will cross where the Fane sends out the fork to the north. We'll be almost a kilometre apart but we want to be sure we don't fire on each other by mistake. You have your radio. Only use it in an emergency. It's on an unused frequency, but if something happens the Brits may well start frequency-hopping on the off chance of listening in on us. We can't let them suspect our numbers – that's the key to the whole plan. We'll be the biggest and best-armed unit for miles around, so even if we run into something unexpected, there's no need to panic. We'll just blow it away.'

'I wasn't thinking of panicking,' Lynagh said coldly.

'I know, Seamus, but the instinct has always been to hit and run because up to now we've always been outnumbered and outgunned. This time we have the staying power to fight it out toe to toe with the bastards. If you hit something, bring up the M60 and level it.'

'And the escape routes?'

'The cars will be ready and waiting for us, six of them. Once the op is accomplished we pile in and put our foot down. The West Belfast Brigade is expecting us – they have three safe houses ready. We'll lie low for a few weeks before coming home.'

'I still think it would be a hell of a lot simpler to just duck back across the border, Eugene.'

'That's what the bastards will be expecting. And so will the Gardai. Remember they have this place under surveillance even as we speak. If we come running back across the Fane with guns in our hands then we'll be clapped in cuffs. No; we'll do what no one expects – head north. All the shit will be hitting the fan in Cross. They won't be expecting a move in the opposite direction.'

Lynagh nodded, and then said casually: 'What about the Fox? I take it he's in one of your ASUs?'

Finn laughed. 'No, Seamus, he is not. The Fox is a maverick. We give him back-up sometimes, but he doesn't like operating with a big bunch like this. No, he's in Cross at the minute, and he'll stay there.'

'We could do with him on this trip, so we could.'

'It's not his kind of show,' Finn said sharply.

Twenty-four men carrying duffle bags left the pub at irregular intervals through the late evening. They scattered, making their way to a dozen prearranged locations, where they changed into their overalls and Balaclavas, buckled on their webbing and rucksacks, and hefted their weapons. Then individually, in the dark, they made their separate ways to the banks of the Fane. The monitoring Gardai Special Branch officers were lost in the maze of fields and woods and streams that interlocked all along the border. They could not even be sure of the numbers of the men involved, for the IRA had recruited a score of other sympathizers as decoys. They knew that something big was in hand, but as a result of delays, misunderstandings, and plain distrust, this information would not reach British Intelligence until it was too late.

The boat was there, a long, open craft with a single, sputtering outboard, although tonight it was operating under muscle power. Lynagh's brigade rowed it out into the middle of the river, the light of the stars glinting off the rippled water. It was not as dark as the night before and the terrorists could see the shadowy tangle of alder and willow that grew along the banks.

The boat scraped against the northern bank, and the Monaghan Brigade of the IRA disembarked on the soil of Northern Ireland. The boat shoved off, and now the little outboard sputtered into life and put-put-putted away to pick up Finn's brigade. The Monaghan men sat tight, Lynagh peering at the luminous dial of his watch every so often. They had to wait and give Finn's men time to cross before starting out themselves.

Finally, after what seemed an interminable time, the radio uttered a single squash of static. Lynagh nodded to himself and then gestured to the heavily armed men in the trees all around him. The three ASUs shook out and began trekking north to their objective. A kilometre away, Finn's men were doing the same.

9

Lieutenant Boyd rubbed his tired eyes and stared yet again out into the starlit darkness of the summer night. He could see little but the vast dark expanse of Armagh and then Louth rolling out in a broad valley beneath him, now and then punctuated by the twin lights of a moving car. There were no other lights for miles. It was a lonely, God-forsaken place.

Tonight. They had to make their move tonight. His men were all on edge – he could feel their mood as clearly as he could feel his own tiredness. They lay in a rough circle within the banks of the ancient ring-fort, invisible in the darkness underneath their scrim nets and other camouflage.

Gorbals tapped him lightly on the shoulder and offered him an AB ration biscuit with some processed cheese on top. 'Cheese possessed' the men called it. They had eaten nothing but cold tinned food since leaving Bessbrook, and the 'compo' was already having an effect. Boyd's bowels would not move for days, and when they did, the result would be spectacular. He took the biscuit nonethless, nodding at his troop sergeant.

It was like being in a circle of wagons waiting for the Indians to ride up. Boyd did not like the formation he had chosen for the multiple, but since they could not be exactly sure of the IRA approach route, he had decided that all-round defence was the safest bet. If he had had more intelligence on the enemy approach he would have posted cut-offs to thwart any escape and a main 'killing group'. That way there would be no survivors. For the hundredth time, he wondered if he had been wise. They would look bloody fools if the Provos slid past them in the dark and hit their target while all of Ulster Troop were stuck up on a hill with their thumbs up their bums.

For some reason he thought of the undercover agent in Cross, Early. A dour character, no doubt nursing all kinds of chips on his shoulder. Boyd would not have had his job for all the world. It was one thing to be here, in uniform with a rifle in his shoulder and his men all about him, quite another to be alone and virtually defenceless in the enemy heartland. Yes, Early must be having a miserable time, he thought, having to play a role all the time for those Fenian bastards.

Gorbals dug him in the ribs. The little Glaswegian was staring at the Classic monitor. Boyd tensed. The sensors had picked up movement on the lower slopes of the valley. The monitor told him that it was travelling south to north, and that it was more than one man. Then the monitor went still again. The moving men had passed by. That would mean they were on the lower approaches to the hill itself, on the westward side. He found himself grinning at his troop sergeant, and Gorbals grinned back, his white teeth shining in his darkened face.

'Looks like they're on their way, boss,' the Scot whispered.

Boyd nodded. 'Tell the boys. A southern approach, as we thought, but coming up on the western slope. Haymaker's team will hit them first, but wait for my signal.'

Gorbals slithered off to do the rounds of the little perimeter. He was as silent as a snake moving through the harsh upland grass. Boyd checked his Armalite, the familiar adrenalin flush doing away with his tiredness. He felt awake and alive now to his very fingertips, as though his body were hovering a fraction of an inch off the ground, charged with energy. This was it, a chance to wipe out the best brigade the Provos had.

He clicked on the infrared Individual Weapons Sight and peered into a green, brightly lit world. He could see the slopes of the hill clearly, the dark coldness of the trees down by the river – and there, moving up the long slope, tiny bright figures. Four, five, six, eight – at least ten of them. He pursed his lips in a soundless whistle. Cheeky bastards, strolling along as if they hadn't a care in the world.

He tried to make out what weapons they were carrying. He could definitely see an RPG on one man's back, but what was that heavy, stubby weapon another carried?

'Fuck,' he said in a whisper. Some kind of light machine-gun. GPMG or M60.

He crept over to where Haymaker's fire team were lying and whispered in the big trooper's ear.

'One RPG, one MG. Take them out first.'

Haymaker gave the thumbs up and Boyd crept back to his place in the line.

He heard a few faint clicks as safety-catches were set to 'Fire', and brought his own weapon with the infrared sight into his shoulder. He could hear his heartbeat rushing in his throat. Sweat was making his palm slippery on the grip of the rifle, though the night was cool.

The terrorists had fanned out into three bricks. Boyd could see that there were a dozen of them now. The numbers worried him – he doubted now if he could get a hundred per cent kill, and swore silently to himself. Bloody Gardai SB had got their information wrong.

Closer, let them walk closer, into the trap.

'Come on, Paddy,' Boyd found himself whispering. 'Come on – just a little more.'

The terrorists were within two hundred metres now, on the upper slopes of the hill itself. The ground was rocky there, with smaller boulders littering the slope. They could use these as cover, so Boyd wanted to open up at almost point-blank range and take them all out before they could go to ground. If any survived, and made it into cover, things could get messy. He didn't want that; he wanted an operation as antiseptic as the one he had led in Tyrone, as clear-cut as surgery.

That's what I am, Boyd thought: a surgeon, cutting the cancer out of this country.

The lead terrorist paused, and spoke into a walkie-talkie. Boyd sighted on him, and in the instant before he fired he realized something was very wrong.

Why have a radio unless it was to talk to another IRA unit? And the walkie-talkie was small, weak. They must be close by.

All this passed through his mind in a fraction of an instant, but in that instant he had tightened his fist and the Armalite had gone off in a ringing detonation of noise and light. He saw tracer streak out into the darkness. The lead terrorist was blasted off his feet.

All hell broke loose.

The old ring-fort erupted into a fury of automatic fire, tracer cutting criss-cross slashes through the night. Boyd shifted aim as one after another the targets were felled. He saw the RPG man fall along with half a dozen others, all lifted off their feet by the massive impact of the high-velocity rounds.

But he also saw several shapes go to ground, as he had feared. Soon the SAS troopers were receiving return fire, and Boyd was sure he could hear the unfamiliar stutter of the M60.

Earth flew from the banks of the ring-fort as rounds began to go down on their position. Boyd cursed and left the perimeter, seeking out Taff Gilmore, the leader of the fire team farthest away from the enemy. He would get Taff's team to flank the bastards, flush them out into the open, where they would be destroyed.

He found Taff, and above the roar of the fire-fight he shouted instructions in the NCO's ear.

'Approach their position on the left flank. Fire a miniflare when you're in position yourself, and lay down fire. Make the bastards get up and run, Taff. We'll switch-fire as soon as we see your rounds going down.'

Taff nodded, smiling. 'No problems, boss. Lots of the bastards though, aren't there?'

'Too fucking right. Don't let them get away, Taff.'

Suddenly a section of the earth bank next to them seemed to fly up in the air. Boyd was hurled away in a fountain of dirt and stones and landed heavily in the middle of the ring-fort. Groggily, he staggered to his knees, scrabbling for his Armalite.

'What the fuck?'

A second fire-fight had exploded into life on the eastern slopes of the hill. He could see Raymond there, firing short, savage bursts from the second GPMG. Another man was ripping up field-dressings. Two troopers lay inert on the ground, their limbs contorted. One of them was Taff, minus most of one leg. One of the three medics in Boyd's multiple was trying to apply a tourniquet to stem the dark jets of blood that were spurting from the stump of his thigh.

Boyd crawled forward on hands and knees, ears still ringing. It was a full-scale battle now, with the troop blasting away into the darkness and the surviving NCOs issuing fire control orders in hoarse shouts. Someone sent up a Schermuly rocket-flare, and then the night became as bright as day as it lit up the hill and came sailing lazily back down again under its tiny parachute.

Jesus, Boyd thought, still dazed. This is the United Kingdom.

He shook his head and found Gorbals. The Glaswegian was redistributing ammunition.

'The fuckers are on both sides of us, sir!' the little sergeant shouted. 'There's a fucking platoon of them out there, the cunts, and they've got an RPG and at least one MG still operating. Fuckers caught us napping. You all right? You're a right fucking mess.'

Boyd wiped blood out of his eyes.

'I'm fine. Where's the signaller?'

'Whitey's down, boss. Took one in the lungs and the round went right through the 351 too. It's fucked.'

'How are we for ammo?'

'Enough to fight a small war. The bastards aren't coming close – none of the claymores have been tripped.' Gorbals hesitated. 'Are you going to hit the SARBE?'

Boyd thought for a split second. With the 351 gone all they had were the 349s, useless at a range of more than three kilometres in these hills. They were cut off. But to activate the SARBE would be to admit defeat, which was unthinkable. And anyway, a chopper would never be able to land in the middle of a fire-fight. For the moment at least, Ulster Troop was on its own. Besides, this battle would not go unnoticed. There were probably several mobiles on their way even as they spoke.

'We'll fight it out – we don't have a choice.'

Gorbals nodded, satisfied. 'We've three wounded, but the medics can stabilize them for a while. A platoon of them! Southern Special Branch really cocked it up this time.'

And so did I, Boyd thought, but he turned away without saying anything more.

What had been meant as a short, clinical ambush had turned into a messy, protracted battle against superior numbers. The terrorists were not doing a 'shoot and scoot'; they were fighting stubbornly, clearly intent on wiping out Boyd's troopers. It was bizarre. What was worse, it was perfectly feasible, given the fact that the SAS had for once been taken totally by surprise. Already a quarter of Boyd's small force was incapacitated and his perimeter, tiny though it was, was dangerously thin. Boyd hoped the enemy would rush his position; then the claymores would even the score.

He took his place in the line beside Haymaker. The barrel of the GPMG was already glowing a dull red and there was a pile of link and empty cases beside the big trooper. Boyd sighted down his own weapon, but the RPG had broken the infrared sight. He spent precious seconds sliding it off his rifle, and then began firing bursts at the muzzle flashes on the slopes below. The side of Drumboy Hill was stitched with the bright flares of enemy fire, and tracer was zooming up towards the summit of the hill in bright, graceful arcs. One of Taff's fire team was firing his M-79 grenade-launcher with a series of hollow booms, the recoil of the stubby weapon jerking his upper body back savagely. There were explosions, and screams on the hillside below. A ball of flame blossomed in the darkness and there was a whoosh as the RPG answered, kicking up a geyser of dirt and caving in another section of the earth bank behind which the SAS were fighting. Immediately, Haymaker sighted on the place where the RPG had been and fired burst after burst, the linked bullets disappearing into the breech of the GPMG like a rattling snake. Then the MG jammed, and the big man swore rabidly, snapping up the top cover of the weapon to prise free a piece of broken link. Three seconds later the weapon was barking again.

The fighting was furious and incessant. There were several stages to an infantry battle, Boyd remembered. The initial coming under fire, then locating the enemy, and then winning the fire-fight, which meant keeping the enemy's head down. The last stage was the assault. The Provos were intent on winning the fire-fight. When they thought they had suppressed the SAS return fire, they would attack the hill.

Or would they? Boyd didn't know. He was not sure what the men out in the darkness were thinking or planning. He was not even sure of their numbers, except that they were greater, probably twice as great, as his own. One thing was for sure: his men were not winning the battle. They were simply struggling to survive.

At Bessbrook the Greenjacket ops officer put down the telephone, puzzled. He sat and thought for a moment and then abruptly got up and walked out of the almost deserted ops room to find an orderly.

'Tell Lieutenant Grabham to put his men on alert, three minutes' notice to move,' he told the lance-corporal. The man nodded and strode off in the direction of the helipads where Grabham's men, doing their stint as Quick Reaction Force, were killing time in the cool July night. Then the ops officer went in search of his commanding officer.

Lieutenant Colonel Blair was awake at once when the ops officer entered his room. He sat up in bed, rubbing his eyes, his salt-and-pepper hair sticking up. He had been asleep for barely an hour and was still wearing his Norwegian shirt.

'Well, Robert, what is it? Have Boyd's men done their stuff?'

'We don't know, sir. The fact is, we've still no word from them. The RUC have just rung us though and say they've had a local phone in with a report of fireworks being let off in that area – rockets and things. It's hard to say what he saw since no one lives near there, and the locals are so reticent about talking to the RUC at the best of times. This man seems to think that there are some hooligans loose up there with some pyrotechnics, and he says they're frightening his cattle.'

Blair was instantly wide awake.

'You haven't heard anything from Boyd? Nothing at all?'

'Not a cheep since he pressed the squash button to inform us he was in position, sir.'

Blair sucked his teeth, then pinched the bridge of his nose.

'I don't like it. We don't want to compromise Boyd, but if there are a few yobbos out there he may have been compromised already.'

'Surely then he would have contacted us, sir, or even hit the SARBE.'

'Yes, quite . . .'

Blair stood up. 'Fireworks,' he muttered. Then his face went white.

'Send the QRF out now, and warm up two more helis. I want another platoon at the ready within half an hour.'

'Yes sir, But . . .'

'Those aren't bloody fireworks, Robert – that's a fire-fight going on out there. Boyd's in trouble.'

'Sir, he has twelve men out with him.'

'Send the QRF *now*, and ready that other platoon. And alert the RUC in Armagh. We'll want their help in sealing off the area. Have you talked to Major Cordwain yet?'

'No, sir. I came straight to you.'

'Then get him up. He will want to go out with the second QRF. Go, Robert!'

The ops officer left hurriedly. Colonel Blair stood in his socks for a second, shaking his head.

'Christ,' he said. 'The young fool.'

They were running low on ammunition. It said a lot for the enemy's logistics that they were still laying down fire like there was no tomorrow, Boyd thought bitterly, while his own men were down now to two mags apiece and a hundred link for each of the GPMGs. They still had grenades and the 66s though, and the claymores lurked on the perimeter, undiscovered as yet.

He had three wounded on his hands. One was Taff Gilmore, his leg blown off above the knee. He was heavily sedated now, and lay unconscious among the multiple's bergens. Another was Boyd's signaller, Whitey Belsham, shot through the lung. He was sat up to keep the fluid in his chest from drowning him. Blood and mucus stained his face.

The third was Richard Shaw, who had taken a round through the hand. 'Rickshaw' was still on the perimeter, the wounded hand wrapped in field-dressings, his rifle held tightly in his good arm.

All the men still had their Brownings, and three mags each. If the worst came to the worst, they would resort to them.

Before that happened, Boyd had decided to hit the SARBE. Even if a chopper could not land, it would at least inform Bessbrook of what was happening.

The RPG roared again, and there was another explosion on the bank of the old fort. Haymaker staggered back from the perimeter, his hands held to his face, swearing. Boyd crawled over to him.

'Where is it?' he asked the trooper. He had to shout over the roar of the multiple's weapons and the rattle of the attackers' fire.

Haymaker's teeth were clenched tight. 'My eyes, boss. I can't see. I can't fucking see!'

Boyd eased the man's hand down from his torn face, but could see nothing but a mass of dirt and blood and ragged tissue. He handed him over to the medic and then took the trooper's place behind the GPMG. The barrel was white-hot and had set the grass below it on fire. Boyd beat out the flames with his hands, not feeling the burns. Bullets sprayed up the earth around his head and he ducked.

Gorbals scrambled over, and said: 'I'm going to hit the SARBE now, boss.'

Boyd nodded numbly. He felt dazed again. He had failed utterly. All he had succeeded in doing tonight was to lead his men into a carefully crafted IRA ambush.

Gorbals thumped his arm. 'Cheer up, boss – worse things happen at sea!' Then he was gone again.

Responsibility seemed to weigh down Boyd's shoulders. He had been too cocky, too confident in his own and his men's ability. Well, he had paid, and so had Taff and Haymaker and the others.

The night lit up as one of the claymores went off in a flare of blinding light. There were screams that carried even above the gunfire. Then another went off. Both were on the eastern side of the hill. Had the Provos tried to rush the place? Boyd inched forward until he was in one of the battered breaches in the fort's wall.

There were bodies lying there, writhing. Boyd got out a pack of miniflares, fitting one of the little bulb-like objects to the striker and fired it out into the fire-studded night. It soared down the hillside like a missile, and in its light he could see the backs of figures running down the hill.

'Give it to them, boys!' he shouted, elated, and he fired flare after flare down at the retreating figures while his men blasted the last of their ammunition after them, viciously intent on knocking down every one.

The fire-fight sudsided with the dying of the last flare. There were a few random shots but it seemed almost silent after the tumult that had gone before. Boyd's hearing was uncertain, still buzzing with the din of the battle, but he cocked his head and heard a welcome sound borne on the night breeze.

Helicopters.

Gorbals was beside him, his face streaming with sweat.

'Looks like the cavalry have arrived, boss.'

'Too fucking right.'

It was over, Boyd realized. They had survived. He felt a wave of tiredness and relief, closely followed by utter dejection.

'I fucked up, didn't I, Gorbals?' he said to his troop sergeant.'

The Glaswegian smiled. 'I'll let you know that, boss, after we've had a body count. I wouldn't be a bit surprised if we topped a dozen of the wee fuckers tonight. And we're all still here, battered maybe, but alive. So buck up!'

Gorbals slapped him on the shoulder and then was off to do his job: counting remaining ammo, seeing to the wounded, checking the perimeter. The men were lying amid piles of glistening brass cartridge-cases. There was a heavy smell of cordite and blood and broken earth hanging over the hill like a fog. Down in the valley, the choppers were touching down, but up on Drumboy Hill the only sound for a while was the harsh liquid rattle of Belsham's breathing as he fought to get air into his ruptured lung. Boyd bent his head between his knees and was quietly sick.

10

It had been very good, Early thought. He had forgotten how good it could be.

It was not yet dawn, and Maggie lay asleep in his arms, her chestnut hair spilling on to his chest. She whimpered sometimes in her sleep, as though she were having bad dreams, and once she had wept silently, but now she was still.

Early was wide awake and alert. His compact Walther pistol was behind the cistern; he had stashed it there when he went to the loo. It was the only way he could do it without Maggie seeing – she had stuck to him all day like glue. And all night, he remembered, smiling into the still-dark room.

She was an eager lover. His lips still felt raw and he was sure her nails had carved red lines down his back. But for all that she had been almost totally silent. Necessary when living in her brother's house perhaps. It had not cramped her style, anyway.

Apart from the little matter of the pistol, Early was a shade less worried. No matter how consummate an actress she might be, he did not think she suspected him any longer of being a Fred. All to the good – perhaps now she could convince Finn and the South Armagh Brigade.

In fact, it sounded as though they were willing to let him in at the ground floor, from what she had said. Early smiled again. Yes, it was all going well.

There was a hammering downstairs at the back door. Early tensed and Maggie stirred sleepily. He heard Brendan's door open and then a step on the landing, creaking down the stairs. There was a commotion, a series of thumps, men's voices. Early shook Maggie gently by the shoulder.

'Maggie, something's up.'

She was awake in a second, her eyes round and staring.

'Go back to your room, Dominic.'

He looked at her hard face a second, then she smiled. 'Go on – Brendan's a bit protective of his wee sister.'

More voices downstairs. Then someone cried out in pain.

'What's going on? Do you know?'

She was out of bed and reaching for a dressing-gown, her superb breasts swinging as she bent.

'Maybe you'd better come down too.' She looked suddenly haggard, tired, though when asleep her face had been wholly peaceful.

Early pulled on some clothes and followed her downstairs warily. There was no time to retrieve the gun – he would have to trust her. He hoped he was not walking into an IRA interrogation.

Though the sun was beginning to come up and there was a grey light outside, all the curtains in the public bar were tightly closed. There was a group of men in there, and a familiar smell which Early at once identified as cordite. Weapons lay all over the floor, among them a couple of G3s, an Armalite, an AK47, even a spent RPG.

'Jesus Christ,' he said to himself.

Brendan Lavery was in his dressing-gown, his eyes wide

with fear. 'God love us, Eugene, you can't do this to me. You'll ruin me. The peelers'll be here any minute. Jesus, Mary and Joseph.'

'Shut your mouth, Lavery,' Finn said savagely. He was covered in earth and mud. His hands were red with blood and they clutched a G3 that stank of recent firing. He looked almost unhinged.

'My men are hurt. You'll fucking help them or I'll burn this place down round your ears. Seamus!'

Another battered-looking man who was peering out behind a curtain turned.

'It's all right, Eugene. The square's quiet, but there's all sorts going on over at the base. Helicopters and everything.'

Finn laughed harshly. 'Stupid fuckers. We drove up the Cullaville road, right under their bloody noses. They've got troops galore pouring down to the south. They won't look in this direction for a while, so they won't.' He saw Early standing there beside Maggie and the muzzle of the G3 came up.

'What the fuck is he doing here?'

'He lives here,' Maggie snapped at him. 'He's all right, Eugene. He's on our side.'

'On our side,' Finn sneered. He looked round the crowded bar. The place looked like the aftermath of a battlefield, which in a way it was. There were fourteen IRA men there, three of whom were groaning on the floor while their comrades tried to staunch their wounds. The rest looked shocked, dull-eyed but dangerous. Early knew the look. These men had just come from a fire-fight. But where? South, Finn had said. Probably somewhere along the Fane valley, the area Maggie had been sweeping with her binoculars the day before. He cursed himself. While the IRA strike had been going on, he had been in bed with her. Had she planned it that way?

'Brits coming into the square!' Lynagh hissed from the door.

'Lights off,' Finn barked, and Maggie obliged. The bar was silent but for the harsh breathing of the wounded. They heard the distinctive whine of army Landrovers outside.

Brendan Lavery was saying a whispered Hail Mary. Finn glared at him and he went quiet. Headlights swept the windows as the vehicles outside turned. Then the engine noise faded as they drove past the pub.

'They're heading down the Dundalk Road,' one of the terrorists said.

'Stupid fuckers are sealing off the border,' Finn told him, and he smiled, looking diabolical. Early had an urge to throw himself at the man's throat, but he stood stock-still.

The square was quiet again.

'What's the time?' Finn demanded.

'Just gone four,' Maggie told him, and he nodded grimly.

'Still quiet, then. Don't get your knickers twisted, Brendan. We just want to get these lads patched up a bit and then we'll be on our way.'

'Patched up!' Brendan was looking with despair at the bloodstains on his carpet. 'Jesus, Eugene, these boys need a hospital, not an Elastoplast.'

'Shut up, Brendan.' It was Maggie. 'Boil up some water and get out the first-aid kit. It's well stocked. And get some blankets and towels.' Then she turned to Early. 'What about you, Dominic – do you know anything about first aid?'

Early had been trying to work out a way to contact the Security Forces discreetly. Here was the bulk of two IRA brigades just waiting to be snapped up, the Border Fox among them perhaps. He raised his head.

'I . . . I did a course, a long time ago, for the building work, like.'

'Then give me a hand. For God's sake, Eugene, what happened?'

Finn sank down on a chair and set the G3 between his knees. Some of the tension seemed to leave him.

'They were waiting for us. The bastards were waiting for us, but we gave a good account of ourselves. I think we got half a dozen of them.'

Early was kneeling by one of the prone terrorists. The man had taken a bullet through the fleshy part of the thigh, leaving a huge exit wound. He could see the femoral artery laid bare in the torn flesh, pulsing delicately.

'What about you? How many of you were hit?' he asked.

Finn eyed him narrowly. The image of McLaughlin's corpse flashed across his mind. He said nothing.

Brendan was heading for the front door with a mop and bucket.

'Where the hell do you think you're going?' Lynagh asked him.

'To mop the step. There's blood all over it. Now that it's getting light the Brits'll see it.'

'Let him go, Seamus,' Finn ordered, and the stout publican slipped out the door to begin his work.

Maggie was splinting the shattered arm of another terrorist. The man groaned and wept as she straightened the limb.

'Brendan's right, Eugene. You have to get these fellas to a hospital.'

'We're taking them to the Royal.'

'That's bloody miles away!'

'We'll put it about that these are punishment shootings – they're all limb wounds anyway. Somebody shopped us, Maggie, and I intend to find out who.'

'Why Belfast for God's sake?'

'It's the last place they'll look. We'll give these boyos false Belfast ID, throw them into the Royal, and no one will be any the wiser. The Brits will be turning Armagh inside out and all the time we'll be lying low up in the city.'

Gingerly, Early bound up the ripped leg of his patient. He was a trained medic, like many SAS troopers, but he did not do too professional a job, both because he didn't want to arouse suspicion, and because he wanted the Fenian shit to suffer. Inwardly though, he was jubilant. He would get word through to Cordwain then that Finn and his cohorts were in Belfast. It shouldn't prove too difficult to track them down. They were as good as behind bars already.

'I want you to get word to our mutual friend, Maggie,' Finn was saying. 'Tell him to step up his activity and keep the pot boiling down here. In fact, tell him to shoot the shite out of every mobile he sees. We've got to keep them on the hop.'

Maggie nodded without looking up from her work. Finn turned to Early.

'Sure, that's a great job you're doing there, Dominic, so it is. Anyone would think you were Florence Nightingale if you weren't such an ugly bastard.'

Early looked him in the eye.

'I didn't bargain on getting into this sort of thing, Eugene. It scares me, so it does – people running about with guns and all. And look at the state of these poor lads.'

'That's war,' Finn told him. He was regaining his smooth self-confidence.

'We've taken worse casualties tonight, I'll be honest with you, Dominic. There are good men lying dead out there in the fields that could have been safe at home now. But they died for Ireland. God have mercy on them, they died for freedom.'

Early had to bow his head to hide the contempt and hatred on his face.

'We stood up to those bastards and fought them face to face, man to man. And we beat them! Just as free men fighting for their liberty will always beat dictator-led mercenaries in the end.'

Some of the unwounded terrorists were nodding and smiling at Finn's words. Others were silent, taciturn, perhaps remembering the carnage of Drumboy Hill. Dupes, convinced by empty rhetoric, Early thought. He did not believe Finn's claims. If the IRA men had been so successful they would not be in here now, bleeding all over the floor.

'Hurry up there, Maggie,' Finn said, suddenly business-like again. 'We want out of here before the sun's too high. They'll be throwing roadblocks up everywhere. Seamus, what's the time?'

'Quarter past four.'

'Then the transits will be here in a minute. Give us a hand here, Dominic. Seamus, get a man to look out at the back. Come on, Rory, for fuck's sake – pick up your gun.'

The terrorists shuffled or were carried through to the back of the pub. The door was opened and grey early-morning light flooded in. The sun was still but a glint on the rooftops. They could hear helicopters.

An engine was turning over softly. There was a van parked in the backyard emitting blue smoke from its exhaust. The wounded men were loaded onto it, hands placed across their mouths to stifle screams from the rough handling. Another van backed into the yard, the driver puffing furiously on a cigarette, looking half mad with fear. The rest of the IRA men piled in, their weapons banging against the sides as they crowded the interior. Finn beckoned Maggie over for a word. Early could not catch what they were saying, but he saw her nod and then violently shake her head. Finn gave Early a quick, hard glance, and then ducked into the back of the van. Early and Maggie slammed shut the doors and then the vans were off, ticking away into the morning. Something clinked at Early's feet and he bent to pick up a bullet: 5.56mm.

Sloppy bastards, he thought.

Maggie leaned against him. He could smell the fresh shampoo fragrance of her hair. There was blood on her hands.

'Will they make it?' he asked lightly.

'If anyone will, he will. Eugene's a born survivor. Sometimes, Dominic, I think he's a wee bit mad, you know.'

Early laughed.

Brendan padded out into the yard, dressing-gown stretched tight around his ample middle.

'In the name of God, will you get in here? We have to try and clear up the mess. Jesus, Mary and Joseph, I'll end up in the Maze yet. And you, Dominic – I'm sorry you had to see all this. I don't know what you'll think of us – you with your work to go to this morning too.'

They went inside, where it still smelled of cordite and gun oil, fresh soil, sweat and blood.

'Maybe I'll just stay closed today,' Brendan said helplessly, surveying the wreckage of bandages and mud and bloodstains.

'You will not,' his sister told him sharply. 'You'll open up as bloody usual, and you'll have a smile on your face the whole day. Do you hear me, Brendan?'

The rotund landlord nodded numbly and then groped behind the bar for a brandy. Maggie led Early out into the kitchen.

'Thank you, Dominic. You're true blue, so you are.' She kissed him on the lips. 'There's many a man would have panicked or run off when he saw what you saw this morning, but you got stuck in.'

'So did you. I'd nearly think, Maggie, that this wasn't the first time.'

She looked at him but said nothing for a long moment.

'You're in it now, whether you like it or not,' she said in a harder voice at last. 'Eugene doesn't trust you yet, so you'll have to win him over. But I'll fight your corner, don't worry. And Dominic . . .' she paused. 'Don't you be going off anywhere for a while now, you hear me? You don't want to go getting people worried. There's a leak somewhere, you see, and we have to find out where it is.'

'Who it is, you mean.'

'Aye. I can't abide traitors. Whoever he is, he'll get what's coming to him in the end though. We have our own kind of justice down here.'

'I'm sure you do,' Early said, and hugged her lithe body close to him. He had seen the strange look in her eyes, and knew he was not out of the woods yet.

Maggie pulled away, laughing oddly. 'Oh, I'm sorry, Dominic. I forgot about my hands. Look at the mess – you're covered with blood. You'd think you had been shot yourself, so you would.'

11

The SAS troopers filed into their Portakabin wearily. It had been a long night, and a longer morning it seemed. The debrief had lasted for hours, but now it was over at last. All they wanted now was to wash and get some sleep.

Gorbals McFee strode into the cramped space full of metal bunk-beds and piles of military clothing and equipment. The men of the troop were moving like sleepwalkers. They had been keyed up and still raring to go when the helis had brought them back to Bessbrook, but now reaction and the strain of the past two days were setting in. They would sleep for fourteen hours apiece once they got their heads down.

'Listen in, lads,' the little Glaswegian NCO told them. 'We've news from Dundonald on our blokes.'

'How are they, Sarge?' Raymond asked. 'What about Haymaker's eyes?'

'Och him, the big ponce. All it was was a bit of gravel that mucked up his face. It was the blood that had blinded him.'

The SAS men laughed with relief. Haymaker was a popular figure in the troop.

'So he'll be back with us soon, then?'

'He'll be flown back tomorrow, but for tonight he's prob-ably getting a blow-job from some wee nurse.'

'What about Taff and Whitey, Sarge?'

'And Rickshaw,' someone added.

'Taff's leg is gone above the knee. He'll be invalided out, but they can do great things with artificial limbs these days. Rickshaw's hand is a bit of a mess – tendons and everything blown to fuck – so it may not be much use to him. We'll have to wait out on that one. And Whitey, he'll be fine. Might even make it back to the Regiment in a few months, though I don't know what his wind will be like.'

'What was the body count in the end, Sarge?' a trooper asked. 'How many of the cunts did we nobble?'

Gorbals grinned. 'Seven blown away for good, and the Greenjackets picked up three more who were hiding in bushes and full of holes.'

There was an outburst of laughter and back-slapping among the six troopers.

Gorbals held up a hand. 'We hit more of the bastards – they picked up at least two blood trails leading to Clonalig, but the Greenjackets let them slip through their fingers.'

'Crap-hats,' someone said disgustedly.

'There were at least two dozen of them, Sarge. That means there's still a dozen or so of the fuckers at large, armed to the fucking teeth.'

'I know, Wilkie. The Green Machine is sealing off the border even as we stand here. A fucking mouse couldn't creep across to the Republic at the moment without being spotted. Once they try and cross, we'll get them.'

'If they haven't got across already. I'll bet the fuckers are in some pub in the South now with their feet up, having a pint and being treated like shagging heroes.'

'Clonalig,' said Robinson, one of the more thoughtful of the troopers. 'That's north of Drumboy. So they didn't try to head south straightaway, anyway. Why's that, Sarge?'

Gorbals shrugged. 'My guess is they had transport arranged up there. Remember, they were on their way north to do a hit, maybe on Cross itself. They probably piled into a couple of cars and fucked off.'

'Well, we took out ten of them. Shit, that's better than Loughgall.'

'I think it's worth a few beers, lads, once we've had some gonk.'

'What do you reckon, Sarge? Can the NAAFI stretch to a few crates for us?'

Gorbals smiled. 'Aye, sure it can.'

'What's up, Sarge? You don't look so pleased. It's scratch ten of the bad guys!'

'That's right, lads, but there are those' – he jerked one thumb towards the ceiling – 'who think that the whole thing was a bit of a fuck-up.'

'You're kidding! Who?'

'The CO of the Greenjackets for one, and our own Major Cordwain.'

'What's their problem? We did the business, didn't we?' Wilkie protested.

'Aye, but there's some kind of argument over intelligence and sources and all that bullshit.'

'What, you mean the bod we have in Cross?'

'Aye. I think they're worried about him.'

Lieutenant Boyd sipped his tea. It was ludicrous, he thought. Here he was sipping tea from a china cup while still wearing torn and muddy combats. There was blood on his shoulder, from Haymaker's wound. It had dried into a thin black crust.

'I still can't see the problem,' he said.

Cordwain sighed. Outside, helicopters were coming and going like buses, ferrying troops all along the border. Bessbrook was a hive of activity; the resident battalion was pulling out all the stops in its effort to seal the border. But Cordwain knew that it was in vain. The birds had flown the nest.

'It's a stupid, inter-service thing. MI5 have finally cottoned on to the fact that we've poached one of their agents.'

'He's SAS too,' Boyd pointed out.

'Technically, he's been seconded to the Intelligence Service. He's theirs. And now they think we've compromised him, placed him at risk. They want him out.'

'How the hell have we compromised him?' Boyd asked angrily.

'We acted prematurely. Yes, it was a largely successful operation, but not completely so. We only got half of the players involved. The other half are still at large, and probably casting about for the tout who betrayed them. Early's life is in danger because our own action wasn't complete enough.'

'Christ, we took out ten of them, didn't we? It's not our fault that the Southern SB miscalculated their strength.'

'I know that, Charles, but you can see their point, surely. Early must be extracted. We've damaged the South Armagh Brigade, perhaps irreparably, and that's excellent. But the Border Fox is still at liberty, and he was our main target. Intelligence believes that he will now step up activity to cover for the weakness of the Armagh bunch. He's a loner, so he needs no support from them.'

'Are you telling me we're back where we started?' Boyd asked, incredulous.

'In a way, yes.'

Boyd was bitter. It was true that the operation had been scrappy, a seat-of-the-pants job that could all too easily have ended in disaster, but by and large he had been beginning to see it as a great victory. His OC seemed to be treating it as a thing of little account.

'Don't get me wrong, Charles,' Cordwain went on. 'I think the men behaved magnificently. Their conduct throughout the operation was in the finest traditions of the Regiment. But it was also rather a half-baked affair, you have to admit. I take the blame too, for allowing it to go ahead.'

Boyd shook his head wonderingly.

'But we got *ten* of them.'

'I know, but MI5 believes that we were too gung-ho. They think that if we had given Early more time we could have bagged the whole bunch, and maybe the Fox to boot, and all without a messy fire-fight or friendly casualties.'

'That's bullshit. Those bastards weren't wandering around the countryside with M60s just for the exercise. They were going to hit something, and hit it hard. We put a stop to that.'

'I know, I know.'

'What about Early? Does he know yet he's to be extracted?'

'No. We're trying to think up a way to get word to him. The DLB system is far too dangerous now. It'll have to be live.'

Boyd paused with his teacup in mid-air.

'What if Early refuses to come out?'

'I don't know what you mean.'

'Isn't he in a better position to judge whether or not it's too dangerous for him to remain? I don't think we should throw away such a useful agent so quickly. He may not be suspected by the locals. The Cross OP says he's involved with one of the local women, a sympathizer herself. It could be he'll weather the storm.'

Cordwain looked doubtful.

'Don't you think, James, that this is just MI5's way of fucking us around for poaching in their preserve – and getting results by doing it?'

Cordwain chuckled. 'You may have a point there, Charles. What do you suggest, then?'

Boyd stood up and began striding back and forth across Cordwain's office. Mud dropped in clods from his boots.

'Let me set up a meeting with Early, meet him face to face. We'll use the LLB method – I'll sign out a Q car.'

'Your accent isn't up to snuff,' Cordwain warned him.

'It'll do.'

'No, Charles, it won't. We can't afford a fuck-up at this stage. I'll do it. I'll call in at that bar where Early stays. It's about time the place was checked out anyway. And I want you to detail another fire team for possible OP duty. It's time the team in Cross was relieved; and if Early does stay in, then we'll want to keep an even closer eye on him.'

Boyd nodded reluctantly, and yawned.

'Christ, I'm tired.'

'You should get some rest. I'll see you're not disturbed for the next twelve hours. Leave everything to me.'

Boyd nodded, looking suddenly haggard. It was as if the last of the remaining adrenalin from the battle had finally leached out of him, leaving him limp and drained. Cordwain clapped the young officer on the shoulder.

'Chin up, Charles. You won a victory last night, and what-ever the goons say, the troopers think you're Genghis Khan come again. And that's the most important thing. The men trust you with their lives.'

But Boyd, remembering the fire-fight on the hill, could recall only his own bewilderment and despair. It had been luck, and the fighting quality of the SAS trooper, that had pulled them through. His own decisions had all been wrong. He wondered how many of the men knew or suspected that. Gorbals did, at any rate. The little Glaswegian had been distant ever since their return to Bessbrook.

Boyd's mind was going round in circles. He took his leave of Cordwain and shambled down the narrow corridor to the Officers' Mess: a grand name for a collection of tiny, window-less rooms.

He would not make the same mistakes again.

The vehicle checkpoint had slowed traffic on the Dundalk road to a crawl. The rain had started in, darkening the evening so that it seemed more like autumn than summer. The soldiers stood in the road or crouched in the bushes nearby with their SA-80s in the shoulder and the rain drip-ping from the brim of their helmets. Two RUC constables, armed with Heckler & Koch 9mm sub-machine-guns, and bulky body armour, stood with the soldiers and flagged down the advancing cars with a red torch. They had been there since mid-afternoon, checking every vehicle headed south.

There had been rumours all day of a fire-fight down on the border, a real epic affair with a dozen players taken out. Some of the soldiers had been approached by journalists, but they had already been warned not to say anything by their OC. A statment would be issued soon, they were told.

There had been a lot of 'sneaky-beaky' stuff going on lately, and they, the Green Army, were excluded from it. Probably the SAS had been headhunting again, grabbing the headlines while they, the humbler foot-soldiers, did the donkey-work. Bloody typical.

One of the soldiers in the hedge stared darkly into the optic of his weapon's sight. Through the rain and gloom he could see the Irish Republic, not five hundred yards away. It was raining there, too – the weather did not take borders into account.

Despite his Gore-tex waterproof, just issued, he was wet and uncomfortable. Rain trickled down his neck and sleeves as he kept his rifle at the ready, and his boots were full of water from the ditch he crouched in. The bulky Kevlar armour he wore made his torso seem twice as bulky as it really was. He blew a droplet of water from the end of his nose and wondered how much longer there was to go. He was dying for a cup of tea.

Suddenly he was on his side, in the muddy water of the ditch. He found it hard to breathe. What happened? he thought. Did I slip? His legs would not move.

There was shouting all around him, and now he could hear the sharp crack of gunshots, flashes illuminating the wet evening. Christ, he thought, we're under fire. But when he tried to get up his body would not respond. He was numb.

Someone splashed into the ditch beside him. Another soldier, breathing heavily. The barrel of his rifle was steaming in the rain.

'Jesus fuck . . . Corp! Kenny's hit!'

The second soldier yanked a first field-dressing from the pocket on his arm and applied it to his fallen comrade's chest.

'Get me some more fucking dressings here!'

Another soldier splashed over and ripped open a first-aid bag. The pair of them began working on the soldier named Kenny who lay motionless in the calf-deep water of the ditch.

'Kenny, look at me! Can you hear me? Hang in there, man – the heli's on the way. Fucking hang on, you bugger – don't you let me down.'

Kenny felt cold. It was the water, he decided.

So I was shot, the thought came. Bloody hell, I didn't feel a thing.

It had gotten very dark, he thought. He could hardly see his comrades' faces. And it was so cold. Why don't they get me out of this bloody ditch, on to the road? The answer came: cover. Bloody fire-fight going on, and I'm lying on my back. Just my luck.

It had become very dark. He could hear his friends speaking, shouting. Now they were dragging him on to the wet tarmac of the road at last. They were pummelling him with their fists, but it all seemed so far away. He drifted off, their voices fading into silence.

'We've lost him, Corp.'

The soldier knelt in the road with the body between his knees. He had taken off his helmet to give heart massage and the rain had plastered hair all over his face.

The RUC men were holding up the traffic. The three soldiers clustered round the body of their comrade. It lay in a pool of rain-pocked blood, the Kevlar body armour torn open and the shattered chest a mass of field-dressings and clotted gore.

The corporal shook his head, wiped his nose on the back of his hand and retrieved his helmet.

'Nobody got him?'

They all shook their heads.

'He was firing from the Republic, I'm sure of it. I thought I saw the flash. Just that one shot, and then he bugged out. The Fox, had to be.'

'Then there's fuck-all we can do about it, is there?'

The corporal wiped his eyes and then barked angrily: 'Well, don't just fucking stand around in a huddle! What about fire-positions? Jesus Christ. Thompson, where's that bastard helicopter?'

'ETA two minutes, Corp. It's having problems with the weather.'

'Fuck the weather. Fuck the rain. Fuck this whole shitty country! Pete, get a poncho out; cover Kenny up, for God's sake.'

One of the soldiers dug a waterproof sheet out of his webbing and spread it over the corpse lying open-eyed on the road.

The men looked up at the overcast sky. They could all hear it now: the thump of a helicopter negotiating the low cloud.

The corporal of the fire team joined one of the RUC constables in the road.

'Will you look at them, the scum,' the policeman was saying, white with fury. He was looking at the line of cars. The occupants were grinning and laughing, and the driver of the first car stuck his arm out of his window and gave the V for victory sign. The corporal abruptly strode up to the car and leaned close to the driver's window.

'Something funny, mate?'

The occupant, a man in his twenties, looked at him scornfully and then stared straight ahead, whistling.

The soldier swung the butt of the SA-80 and smashed the driver's window with an explosion of glass. Then he leaned in, opened the door, and dragged the driver out of his car.

'Think it's funny, do you? Thinks it's something to laugh at, a man dying on the road? *Think it's fucking funny now?*'

The corporal kicked the man in the stomach, and he collapsed on to the ground. He kicked him again, in the face; and again, and again. Then he leaned over the groaning, bloody civilian and put the muzzle of his rifle in the man's mouth. The eyes widened with terror and the man moaned around the barrel.

'Not so fucking hilarious now, is it, you piece of shit?'

There was a roar, and a high wind that drove the rain horizontally. The helicopter was landing in a field by the road. The corporal straightened and tucked his rifle back in his shoulder. He looked down at the bruised, terrified man on the ground, and smiled.

'The gloves are off now, Paddy. Tell your friends. We're throwing the book away because we've had enough. Now it's your turn.'

He kicked the man once more before turning back to where his fire team were loading the dead soldier's body on to the Wessex.

12

The bar was quiet when Cordwain walked in. It smelled strangely of bleach, he thought. He ordered a Bass from the plump man behind the bar and sipped it thoughtfully. Early should be back from work any minute. After that they'd have to play it by ear.

He was glad the fine July weather had broken; it gave him more of an excuse to wear the jacket which concealed the Browning in his armpit. It was raining outside, a fine drizzle wholly characteristic of South Armagh.

Things were hotting up. Three days had passed since Boyd's operation, and already another soldier had been killed by the Fox. There were signs that the Greenjackets were fed up with taking it lying down; there had been a spate of complaints about army brutality. The local RUC had given the complainants short shrift. In fact there was a rumour that one man, having gone to the local RUC station to complain about being beaten up by the army, had found himself beaten up again by the police. Cordwain smiled unwillingly. The Troop had loved that.

In two days' time a new covert OP would be set up in a derelict house in the square. Gorbals McFee would be handling it. That would make two covert OPs operating primarily to keep tabs on Early. Ulster Troop could not keep up the intensity of operations for long. Soon they would have to scale things down. One thing was for sure, Cordwain told himself: he was not letting a twelve-man multiple out headhunting in the countryside again.

He wondered if Early had any fresh intelligence for him. There had been no contact since the Drumboy op, to let things settle down a little. But Cordwain was seething with impatience. He wanted to know where Finn and the other surviving Armagh and Monaghan players had skedaddled to after their abortive mission. The Gardai reported that none of the Monaghan men had yet returned to their homes, and neither had the Armagh lot. They were lying low somewhere: Donegal maybe, or Mayo. They had slipped through his fingers when he had been on the verge of scooping the whole damn lot up.

But this Fox now – he was the main problem. He had taken out five Greenjackets in less than as many months. No wonder the squaddies on the ground had lost their sense of humour. And yet Cordwain had not one single clue about the formidable sniper, whether he was a Northerner or Southerner, old or young. Intelligence had come up with a great fat blank, which was unusual. Whoever he was, he was not a known player, in fact not even a familiar face. It was irritating.

'Desperate things going on in this part of the world lately,' he said to the barman in his Belfast accent. The man seemed nervous, jittery, and he sipped often at a tall glass of whiskey he had stashed behind the bar.

'Ach, Jesus, don't talk to me about it. It's terrible, so it is. All those young men dying, all this violence; and the soldiers going berserk around here too. I wish it would quieten down. All we want is to be left alone to get on with our lives.

He sounded sincere. Cordwain wondered if he had had some experience lately that had formed his views.

He ordered another pint, looking discreetly at his watch, and then unfolded his *Irish Times* and began reading. The headlines were still full of the news of the Drumboy killings. The paper speculated on whether this was confirmation of the British Government's 'shoot to kill' policy. Cordwain smiled at the absurdity of it. Army Pamphlet No. 1 was actually entitled 'Shoot to Kill', and covered basic weapons handling. When a soldier fired his weapon, he was always intending to kill, never to wound. A wounded enemy could still kill a man. Journalists could be so fucking naive. They had to dance words on the head of a pin.

A girl walked into the bar laden down with shopping. She was highly attractive, Cordwain thought, her hair lank with the rain but still shining chestnut, her face pale as cream. Maggie Lavery, the sister of the landlord. She had been a Sinn Fein member a few years back and was still a sympathizer, but Intelligence said that she had not been actively involved since the death of her husband at Loughgall. The SAS OP observing the house had said that she and Early seemed to have a bit of a thing going.

Lucky Early, Cordwain thought, eyeing the way her wet dress clung to her slim body. He could see the imprint of her nipples through the thin material. The shower must have caught her by surprise.

The girl gave him a glance as she hauled her shopping away through the door at the back of the bar. She looked as haughty as a queen. Cordwain wondered what she saw in John Early, hard-faced, short and stocky. Women were funny things.

The door opened and a crowd of men burst into the bar, talking and laughing. They carried lunch-boxes and their overalls were covered in mud and plaster. They stood at the bar, shaking the rain out of their hair and calling loudly for beer. One of them prevailed upon the landlord to switch on the TV above the bar, and suddenly the racing from Sandown was blaring out at high volume. The men sank their pints with scarcely a pause and then ordered more. The girl came back into the bar, wearing dry clothes now but with her hair still damp, and began helping her brother pull pints. The lounge had been transformed in a twinkling from a quiet, empty room to a bustling, noise-filled place.

And there was Early, entering with a few more labourers. Cordwain saw him catch Maggie Lavery's eye and smile. She smiled back at him, looking not haughty now but girlish. Cordwain felt a twinge of envy, though he was happily married himself.

Early saw him. There was a flicker, almost like a twitch, and then he had turned away, elbowing his way to the bar and calling loudly for beer with the rest.

'You're dinner's nearly ready, Dominic,' the Lavery woman was telling Early. 'I'll fetch it out as soon as I get a minute.'

'Ach, there's no hurry,' Early said, and casually propped himself up beside Cordwain but placed his back to the other SAS officer. He was laughing and joking with the other men in the bar. Cordwain was a little amazed. He had always known Early to be a taciturn, humourless type, but he seemed to have the locals eating out of his hand.

Time for business. Cordwain nudged Early slightly with his elbow and the shorter man turned, pouring the last of his beer down his throat. Cordwain got up as if to leave.

'Are you finished with your paper?' Early asked him. 'It's just I like to have a wee look at the horses, so I do.'

'Aye, no problem. It's yours,' Cordwain said casually, and he left the bar.

Still raining. He turned up his jacket collar and headed for the car park, where he had left the Q car. Written in the newspaper he had left with Early were the time and place for a live letterbox rendezvous that night. That was if Early could tear himself away from his flame-haired beauty.

The weather really had taken a turn for the worse. Cordwain switched on the windscreen wipers and peered out at the rain-swept evening. He looked at his watch. Forty minutes. Should be time enough.

He turned the car down a little side-road and saw a figure waiting at the bottom, hunched up against the rain. When he drew level with the man the door was opened and the wet figure leapt into the passenger seat. He sped up.

'I can't be long,' Early said, throwing back the hood of an old army surplus parka. 'They're keeping quite a close eye on me at the minute, I think.'

'The woman?' Cordwain asked.

'I don't know. Maybe.'

'All right,' Cordwain said. 'You first.'

Early paused, as if collecting his thoughts.

'Finn and the other PIRA members are in Belfast, in three safe houses. That's all I know about their location. They took their weaponry with them and they intend to lie low for several weeks, they said, before popping back south. I suppose you've nothing on them?'

'Not a damn thing,' Cordwain said. 'The wounded players we scooped up aren't talking.'

'Finn's a hard case – they're probably more scared of him than they are of you. Any luck with the weaponry?'

'One M60 has been traced to a theft from a National Guard arsenal in the States about eight months ago. The rest came up from bunkers in the South. The Gardai are working on it.'

'The Gardai,' Early scoffed.

'Anything else?'

'Yes. The Lavery woman is active. There is at least one arms cache in the pub itself, but her brother doesn't know, I think. He seems a decent sort. I think he just wants to be left alone.'

'I got that impression.'

'The survivors of the operation came to the pub three – no, four nights ago. We patched them up before they went on their way. They were in two Ford Transits, one blue, one grey. Number-plates are as follows.' Early handed Cordwain a tiny scrap of paper. The SAS major nodded.

'Hijacked in Newry a week ago,' he said. 'One we've found, burnt out along the border near Omagh. That's what threw us off the scent. We thought they had headed west. So they're in Belfast! Cheeky buggers. Tell me about the crowd who made it to the pub.'

'There were fourteen of them. Some I couldn't place. Three of them were wounded: arm and leg injuries. They were to be admitted to the Royal in Belfast with false ID and passed off as punishment shootings.'

Cordwain smiled. 'Scratch three more of the bad guys. We'll leave them alone for the present. We don't want you coming under any more suspicion. The others?'

Early nodded at the piece of paper he had given Cordwain. 'Southern Special Branch will be able to confirm the names.'

'Excellent, John. I believe we have them cold.'

'What the hell happened the other night? You only bagged half of them, and the other half are thirsting for blood. You'll never get any Freds down in this part of the world if you keep coming up with operations like that.'

'It was Boyd. He's a good man, but a little . . . impulsive. Call it one of the follies of youth.'

'Fuck the follies of youth,' Early said savagely. 'He could have ruined the whole thing. I hadn't given you enough information to launch a preemptive strike. I thought you would just step up preventative measures, maybe catch them in the act. That young man is too much of a cowboy.'

'As I said,' Cordwain told him, his voice hardening, 'he's young, but he's very good. It was my fault if anybody's – I gave the go-ahead. Do you think you've been compromised by the operation?'

Early pondered the question as the car wound its way along the quiet roads of South Armagh.

'No,' he said at last. 'I patched up one of their wounded and helped them out the night of the fight. They are on their guard, certainly, but I don't think they suspect me any more than a few other locals that they've got their eye on.'

'And the Lavery woman?'

'What about her?'

'Damn it, John. Is she setting you up? We know you're involved with her, and she's bloody attractive.'

'I won't let my prick rule my head, if that's what you're getting at, James.'

'Good. Now listen, John. Your handlers in the Intelligence Service have found out what we're up to and they're mightily pissed off at us intruding on their turf. They want you extracted. They're trying to portray the Drumboy op in the worst possible light.'

'They're full of shit. I've just given you the whole South Armagh Brigade on a platter.'

'Yes, but they want the Border Fox. The whole situation down here is being screwed up tighter every day, despite Drumboy. The resident battalion is causing trouble for itself, and questions are being asked in Parliament.'

Early laughed. 'How inconvenient for you all!'

'It could result in the Greenjackets being replaced early in their tour – their casualties alone almost warrant that. That would be a grave blow to us, politically as well as operationally.'

'What do you want me to do about it?'

'Find the Fox. He must be taken out before he strikes again. I am able to authorize any and every means to neutralize him once he has been identified. If the worst comes to the worst we'll drag the fucker over the border and top him ourselves. But he must go down.'

'The Fox is mine, Major.'

Cordwain sighed.

'This is not a personal vendetta. I'm sorry about your brother, John, but Christ, you've got to remember you're part of a team. We're establishing another covert OP in Cross square to keep an eye on you. The first one is being folded up – the risk of compromise is too great with two in the same town.'

'Fair enough. I'll tell you this though: we may be on to a loser with the Fox, precisely because he prefers to work alone. Not even the regular players in Cross know who he is – only Finn and the quartermaster, McLaughlin, one of whom is now dead and the other up in Belfast. Whoever he is, he's not in our files – he's an unknown, with no previous convictions. And he's a cool-headed bastard too, hitting that VCP the day after the Drumboy op.'

'We've figured out the weapon he uses,' Cordwain said. 'It's a Barratt-Browning .50-calibre rifle. Uses armour-piercing rounds. The fucker can punch through four inches of steel; it even pierces the trauma plates on body armour.'

Early whistled softly. 'Where the fuck did the Provisionals get a weapon like that?'

'The States, where else? It's American-made. But it's a fuck of a big weapon, John. A man wouldn't be able to run far with it, so this Fox depends on vehicular transport for every hit, if he uses no back-up. That means he operates near roads, tracks, lanes. He's not a cross-country man, unless he's in the Republic, where he can probably saunter around with his hands in his fucking pockets if he likes. Anyway, back to business.'

Cordwain handed Early one of the ubiquitous pieces of paper.

'Three times, dates and places for three LLBs. It's up to you whether or not you turn up at them; there will be a contact waiting for you at them but he will wait precisely five minutes and then bugger off. They're roughly every week for the next three weeks.'

'What if I get info that has to be delivered right away?'

The number at the bottom. Use a public phone box and let us know. If you're really in the shit, then hopefully the OP being established tonight will notice and call in the cavalry. That's the best we can do. Fibre optics and phone taps, they're all out at the moment, I'm afraid; things are too tense. We'll wait a while, and then see what we can do. I don't have to tell you to destroy that note, do I?'

Early shot him a withering look.

'Good. Here we are then, John – back where we started. What did you tell the girl?'

'That I was going for a walk.'

'On an evening like this? You'll have to think up better excuses than that.'

Early said nothing. The car stopped briefly and he got out.

'Good luck,' Cordwain said, and sped off. Looking in his rear-view mirror he saw the hooded figure hunched against the rain, walking back into Cross.

Maggie Lavery or no, he was glad he was not John Early.

13

The army foot patrol was a large one; twelve men in staggered file moving down both sides of the darkened street. It was three o'clock in the morning and the street-lights of Crossmaglen were an amber glow in the early hours. The village was silent and sleeping, but the soldiers checked every window and doorway as though they expected a face to appear at it, a rifle barrel to flash. They were tense, jumpy, and they eyed the death tally that graffiti artists had painted on one gable wall with hatred. Ten-nil, it said, seemingly forgetting the seven PIRA members killed at Drumboy Hill. The thought sweetened the mood of the patrol a little, though they were still burning with a desire for revenge, like all the members of their battalion. Scarcely three days had passed since the murder of rifleman Kenny Philips at the vehicle checkpoint outside the town.

Gorbals McFee and the three other members of his team were at the rear of the patrol. Haymaker was there, the stitches removed from his face only that morning, Raymond Chandler, and Jimmy Wilkins: Wilkie. They were dressed and equipped identically to the Greenjacket soldiers that preceded them, except for the large bergens on their backs. The patrol was to cover their approach to the site of the OP.

On the northern side of Cross square was a line of three derelict houses, their windows boarded up and slates missing from their roofs. The local council had been promising for months to renovate them, but never seemed to get round to it. The patrol turned east on its approach to the square and moved down the narrow alley at the back of the houses. A head-high crumbling brick wall enclosed the tiny, overgrown back gardens. The doors in the wall were of wood, rotting and sagging on their hinges.

A cat darted across the alleyway, causing the point man to whip up his rifle, then breathe out softly and let the muzzle sink again. It was army policy to have weapons loaded but not cocked while patrolling in urban areas, so that there was no round 'up the spout' to cause a possible negligent discharge. But this moral nicety had gone to the wall a long time ago down in South Armagh. All the section's weapons had been cocked as soon as the patrol had left the base, and the trigger finger of each man rested on the little stud that was the SA-80's safety-catch, ready to flick it off and open up at the slightest hint of danger. The Greenjackets had lost too many men to worry much about infringements of Standard Operating Procedure now.

The patrol paused, the men seeking fire-positions. Gorbals nodded to Haymaker and the big man leaned against one of the doors in the alley, testing it. Letting his weapon hang from its sling, he produced a short crowbar from his thigh pocket and levered the door open. The hinges squeaked in protest, and then he had disappeared.

In a twinkling the other SAS men followed him, and the door was swung shut. The Greenjackets continued down the alley and then turned left to enter Cross's main square, on their way back to the base, which was off its southern end.

Gorbals, Raymond and Wilkie crouched in the tangled undergrowth that was the back garden of the deserted house. They were almost invisible in the darkness. Haymaker was working on the garden door, disguising the scar the crowbar had made.

The procedure was repeated for a window at the back of the house. Soon the team was inside, breathing dust and damp in the pitch-blackness.

They went up the stairs, Wilkie erasing their footsteps behind them as they went. No one spoke. When they had reached the top floor they paused, listening. Then they slipped off their bergens and placed them in a pile, and swapped their boots for trainers.

The house had already been checked out by an Explosives Ordnance Disposal team, and the SAS men had clocked both the building and the surroundings on a previous patrol. The place was clean, in an operational sense, though as the SAS soldiers dug out their equipment they could feel rats scampering around their feet.

Each of the men had differing tasks to perform before the OP could begin to function. Haymaker went downstairs again and planted a series of trip-wires linked to stun grenades and flash initiators on the lower floor, so that if any of the locals came nosing around the team would have warning that they were compromised. Wilkie engineered a tiny hole in the brickwork under the eaves that would be their sole window on the world, and began setting up the surveillance equipment. Raymond got out two sleeping bags and unrolled them, and then set aside two sets of plastic bags, one pair for human waste and the other for empty food cans. The team would be in the OP for ten days, and in all that time they would not eat hot food, but only cold, tinned rations. They would not have hot drinks, except at first light, when there was the least chance of the little gas stove being heard. And they would drink tea, not coffee, which gives off an aroma.

Gorbals set up the radio, which would be used as little as possible, both to conserve batteries and cut down on noise. The procedure would be for two men to sleep while one monitored the radio and the fourth carried out the surveillance, logging everything he saw. Radio transmissions from the OP would be made at night only, since the VHF set had a habit of interfering with television transmissions. Every third night, an RGJ patrol would pass close to the OP and pick up a bergen full of waste and used camera films, and would leave behind a bergen full of food, film and radio batteries.

By first light that morning, the OP was up and running. Gorbals was sitting with his eye glued to the optic of the camera, while Raymond sat listening to the radio. Wilkie and Haymaker were asleep, wrapped in sleeping bags on the dust and filth of the floor.

As Maggie Lavery got out of bed and stretched her white arms towards the ceiling, Gorbals smiled and pressed the shutter on the camera. What a great pair of tits, he thought. Surveillance work has its perks, after all.

Eugene Finn lit another cigarette and stared down the rain-shiny roofs of the city. From this height he could even see the two huge yellow Harland and Wolff cranes, Samson and Goliath, over by the docks, as well as the green copper dome of the City Hall. A helicopter hovered, motionless, over Belfast city centre, keeping an eye on things.

He was in a high-rise in Divis, in west Belfast. The IRA safe house had turned out to be a grimy tenth-floor flat in the Republican heartland, the ghetto of the city. Belfast was a grim town, divided up into tribal territorities, split by the Peace Line, patrolled by troops and controlled by paramilitaries. He had never liked the place. He was a countryman.

The door was knocked in a peculiar rhythm and the other man in the room, a big Falls Road native, got up to answer it. He was Seamus Toomigh, Finn's 'minder'. Or jailer, or executioner, Finn told himself. It all depends on how things go.

Six men came into the room, the last looking round the corridor before shutting the door behind him. Finn stubbed out his cigarette. The men sat down and Toomigh wandered off to the tiny kitchen to get drinks. Finn knew the names of two of the men. The other four he did not even recognize.

It was one of the beauties of the ASU system. The IRA Active Service Unit was a self-contained entity, and the foot-soldiers within it knew no one in the organization outside their own little cell. Only the commanders of the ASUs, and the brigade officers knew who the various quartermasters and staff officers of their district were. And only a man who had been in the 'Ra' as long as Finn would know who the men on the Army Council were. This was the bulk of it: these six men. They dictated and co-ordinated the actions of all the IRA members on the island. It was rare to see them all together, especially up here in the North, for the Brits knew who at least a few of them were. Finn knew he would be moved again, to another place, as soon as the meeting was over. The Brits or the RUC would have these men under constant surveillance.

'Well, Eugene,' said one of them, a middle-aged, hard-faced character. He was Francis McIlroy, operations officer for the Belfast district.

'You've been having an exciting wee time to yourself down south, haven't you?'

'Have we now?'

'Seven Volunteers dead, three more in the Royal, some valuable weapons lost. I'd say you'd been busy enough,' another man said harshly. Finn did not know him.

'And for what? Four wounded SAS. You didn't even manage to top any of them. The biggest operation we'd authorized in fifteen years and what have we to see for it? Fuck all. Now the South Armagh Brigade is out of action for the foreseeable future. You know what I think, Eugene? I think you just handed the Brits a victory on a platter, with nothing gained on our side but corpses.'

'What is this?' Finn asked heatedly. 'A trial?'

'Call it a court martial – we prefer that term. You lot in the South have always been a bunch of big-timers. Before you it was Kelly and the East Tyrone Brigade: and look where it got them – that disaster at Loughgall. Who the fuck do you think you are, Clint Eastwood?'

Finn leaned forward, his face white with anger. 'You authorized it. The Army Council backed the idea behind the operation.'

'We backed it before we knew there was a leak in your parish. Someone down there is singing, Eugene. Why else should the SAS be waiting for you?'

Finn was silent. The same thought had occurred to him.

'You Armagh boys have always been the tightest-knit bunch of us all, I'll make no bones about it. But now there's a screw loose, Eugene. Somebody in Cross is a tout.'

Finn shook his head. 'Even the other ASU commanders only knew the details of the operation the night before. I can't see how it could happen.'

'Where are they now? Here?'

Finn smiled icily. 'They're six feet under, most of them. Lynagh is the only one that survived besides me. He's up here in the city. I don't know where you have him – you know that.'

'We'll talk to him too, then. But I don't think it was him or you, Eugene. Don't get us wrong – we don't suspect you yourself.'

Finn felt a cold wave of relief wash over him, but his face betrayed none of his feelings.

'No, it's someone in Cross, and they're good, whoever they are. My guess is they put together a whole lot of little pictures and came up with one big one.'

Finn nodded. 'I think the SAS were as surprised as us. There weren't more than a dozen of them. If they had known how many of us there were, they'd have brought in more. At Loughgall they had over thirty men. The East Tyrone bunch had nine.'

The senior IRA figures digested this for a few minutes while Toomigh came back in with glasses of beer and whiskey.

'Just how bad is the damage?' McIlroy asked at last.

'Bad enough. Two of the dead were mine, the rest were Monaghan men under Lynagh. It was his platoon they hit first . . .'

'*Platoon!*' one of the older men guffawed in a mixture of wonder and admiration.

'Aye. They wiped out half of his men in the first minute, but they didn't seem to know my lot were there. We hit them in the rear, RPG and everything, and we were fucking winning, too, until that arsehole McLaughlin charged forward with a few of the hot-heads, and tripped a booby-trap. A claymore, I think it was. Well, he went down along with a few others, and after that I gave the order to pull out. Three of the wounded we managed to get on the vans, the others were picked up by the Brits. But the point is, we had them surrounded. I really think we could have beaten the cunts if only we'd had a little more time.'

'A dozen SAS – now wouldn't that have been something,' said one of the IRA men, eyes shining. The others were looking at Finn with something like respect.

McIlroy persisted, however.

'How many of your brigade are left, Eugene?'

'Eight. As I said, the Monaghan boys took the brunt of it. The Monaghan Brigade has more or less ceased to exist.'

McIlroy smiled strangely. 'I'll bet you a pound to a pinch of pigshit that the Brits think the South Armagh Brigade is destroyed too. They think all they have to worry about now is the Fox.'

'If there's a tout in Cross they may know I'm here,' Finn warned.

'Sure they do. We'll have to get you and your boys out again as soon as we can.'

'What are you talking about? I thought the plan was that we'd lie low here for a while.'

'You're not safe here any more than you are in Cross, and you're more use to us down there. The Brits want the Fox now – desperately. And they'll not expect him to have any support with you lot up here. If we can use him as bait, then maybe we can get them into an ambush. Have your boys waiting for them – this time without any fuck-ups.'

'I'm not sure my boys will agree,' Finn said quietly.

'They'll obey orders, so they will.'

'I'm not sure the Fox will agree either. He's not a team player.'

'Then you'll convince him . . . Who the hell *is* he, Eugene? You know, don't you?'

'I know, but no one else does. We'll keep it that way, so we will.'

'Aye, it's better that way, I suppose. I'd like to shake his hand though. He's got the shits up every cunt on the border.' And McIlroy laughed.

'There is one thing though,' he added, serious again. 'There will be no more operations down in your area until you weed out this fucking tout. That's your first priority. We'll send you back south first, and I want you to start looking around. The rest of the brigade will follow sometime in the next two weeks. Let the Brits think the Fox is on his own down there. And everything you find out is to be forwarded to the Army Council – no one else. We will handle the situation ourselves, and give you the go-ahead when we're satisfied it won't turn into another fucking shambles. Is that clear?'

'Perfectly,' Finn said, his voice cold as stone.

'Good. We've reached a turning point down in your part of the world, Eugene. The Brits think they have us on the run, so we have to prove them wrong. Tell the Fox to lay off for a while. No more hits until you get word from us. I want things to quieten down around Cross for a few weeks, lull the enemy into a false sense of security. Let them think that they have us beat down there, and then hit them hard, to show them we're still in business.'

Finn nodded wordlessly.

'You don't look too enthusiastic, Eugene.'

'I'm enthusiastic enough. It's the boys I'm thinking of. Half of them will end up in the Maze, if they come through it alive at all.'

'Negative thinking, Eugene, will get you nowhere. Everyone does a stint in the Maze – it's part of the learning process. Thank your lucky stars they don't get sent to Castlereagh any more, and get the cigarette burns and the beatings we used to get, eh lads?'

There was a murmur of agreement from the older of the IRA men.

'And they don't have to smear their shit on the walls and live under a blanket for months on end. They have it easy nowadays, Eugene. No more Dirty Protest, no more hunger strikes. Hell, the Loyalists and us run the Maze between us. The screws don't do anything there without our say-so.'

'I know,' Finn said drily. He had done time in the Maze himself.

'Then what's the problem?'

'This tout. I have an idea who he might be. I just hope I'm wrong, that's all.'

'Why? Who is he?'

Finn smiled. 'A friend of mine is sweet on him. He's a Ballymena man. She's keeping an eye on him, don't worry. He's not going anywhere.'

14

The pub was crowded, hot, smoky. Early leaned against the bar with the cool glass of porter in his hand and surveyed the crowd. So many of the people here he knew, now. Not only from mugshots, but from working with them, drinking with them, even playing football with them at weekends. Gaelic football, that is. They had loved that; a Ballymena man who knew how to play Gaelic. He was a novelty.

His back ached. Eoin Lavery worked his men hard, but was not a bad employer. Early had begun to look forward to the weekends though. They were a respite from early mornings and hard physical labour, and they were a chance for Maggie and him to get away, into the fields. The good weather had returned, and South Armagh was peaceful for the moment. It amused and somehow saddened Early that he could walk this countryside freely now. He had patrolled it, heavily armed, before his transfer to the SAS, and had regarded it as a battlefield where every gate was booby-trapped, every road mined. Now he could enjoy it as a civilian. And the girl; he enjoyed her too.

He drank more of the cool beer, tapping one foot gently against his right ankle to check the automatic was still there in a gesture that had become instinctive. It wouldn't do to forget that he was an alien in this country. He was the enemy.

He had deliberately missed the first of the three LLBs that Cordwain had set up, because he had had nothing to say, and also because he had wanted to let things settle down for a while. At the second he had merely found out the next three locations and times. There was no intelligence forthcoming these days. The country seemed subdued after the battle at Drumboy Hill and the Fox's last killing. According to Cordwain, the three IRA men wounded in the Drumboy fight were doing well in hospital, under discreet surveillance. He doubted if they would be activated again. They would become Republican war heroes, but operationally they were hot potatoes for the IRA. They were out of the picture. That meant that Drumboy had actually taken out thirteen of the fuckers, but according to the Gardai, only four of the thirteen were Northerners. The rest were Monaghan boys. Cordwain had therefore told Early to gather any information he could on those members of the South Armagh Brigade who returned to their old hunting grounds. The RUC had drawn a blank in Belfast, though it was known that there had been a meeting of the IRA Army Council at which at least one of them had been present.

Finn, Early thought. He would have been there. And he'll come back, too, looking for the tout who shopped him. Well, forewarned is forearmed, as they say.

Early's own enquiries, in the form of bar-room banter, had also come up with nothing. Most of the people of Cross preferred to forget about the Drumboy fiasco and concentrate on the continuing triumphs of the Border Fox. It made Early's gorge rise to see these outwardly placid, merry people cheering the murder of soldiers on their roads and in their fields, but he joined in with a will, singing along with the best of them. Damned if they weren't singing now – a bunch of them in the smoke-veiled warmth and crowd of the bar.

Down on the Border, that's where I'd like to be,
Down in the dark with me Provo company;
With a comrade on me left and another one on me right,
And a bunch of ammunition just to feed me Armalite.

A brave RUC man came walking down our street;
Six hundred British soldiers were
tripping round his feet.
He said: 'Come out, ye Fenian bastards,
come on out and fight.'
But he said he was only joking when he
heard me Armalite.

There was a roar of laughter and a torrent of back-slapping as the song finished. Early stared into his glass.

'*Tiocaigh ar la!*' someone shouted. 'Our day will come.' Too fucking right it will, Early thought darkly. If I have anything to do with it, it'll come sooner than you think, you bastard.

Maggie leaned over the bar towards him, cleaning a glass. Her face was flushed with the heat and perspiration beaded her forehead.

'This is a right crowd we have in tonight, Dominic. They're great ones for the songs and the slogans, this bunch, but that's about all they're good for.'

He looked at her blankly, and she squeezed his arm with a smile.

'We know there's more to it than that, don't we?'

He felt a sudden urge to confess all to her, to tell her everything and ask her to forgive him, to accept him, to run away from here with him. The classic dilemma of the undercover agent under pressure. Instead he leaned forward and kissed her lightly on the lips. Her brother Brendan saw the gesture and shouted across the bar: 'Hey, you two – none of that canoodling in here!' but he was grinning. Apparently he had come to consider Early a good egg, someone fit to court his sister.

One other drinker did not share in the general merriment. He was a well-dressed man in a suit, balding and overweight. He was holding on to a pint glass as though his life depended on it and looking at the people around him as though he were a rabbit surrounded by weasels. He drained his glass quickly and left, collecting an expensive overcoat from the hooks by the door and exiting into the July night. Early watched him go, intrigued. Then Jim Mullan, one of his workmates, nodded in the bald man's direction and nudged Early.

'See yon fella, Dominic? He's a Prod. Some of the boys have been watching him. He's nervous as a cat. He's one of them travelling salesmen, he says, but I don't believe a word of it.'

'What do you think, then?' Early asked, trying to sound unconcerned.

'We think he's a fucking spy. I've heard' – and here his voice dropped to a whisper – 'that those poor lads who were murdered at Drumboy were set up by a fucking Brit spy. You know, a secret agent.'

Early widened his eyes in horror. 'No!'

Mullan, a big, florid man with several inches of gut bulging over his belt, closed one eye. 'But don't worry – some of the boys is waiting outside for him, the baldy-headed wee ponce. We're going to have a wee word with him, so we are.'

'What are you going to do to him?'

Mullan winked again. 'Ach, nothing much, maybe give him a wee tap or two and scratch that expensive car of his. Now drink up, Dominic. You're a broad sort of fella – we could do with you out there as well.'

Early drained his pint and followed in Mullan's wake as the bigger man left the bar.

It was a fine night, the stars ablaze in a clear sky as he followed Mullan round to the car park behind the pub. Already an ugly little drama was being enacted there under the soft glow of the street-lights. A tight knot of men were gathered about something. Others were kicking a BMW that sat nearby. There was a tinkle as a headlight shattered. A man screamed in pain. Early's pace quickened.

The salesman was being held by two of Early's workmates while a third beat him about the head with a short iron bar. The man's head lolled from side to side with each blow. The flat, dull crack of the blows sickened Early. Without pause he stepped into the knot of men and snatched the weapon from the attacker.

'What the *fuck* do you think you're doing?' he demanded savagely.

The men looked at him in surprise. Behind him, the salesman slumped in their arms, glassy-eyed and barely conscious. There was a great wound in his head that trickled blood. His new suit was covered in it.

'We're interrogating him,' one of them said lamely.

'Aye – whose fucking side are you on anyway, Dominic?' There was a general growl at this, and suddenly Early knew that he had made a bad mistake. He had let his quick temper get the better of him.

'Now, lads,' big Jim Mullan said. 'Don't forget Dominic's a new boy here. He doesn't know our ways yet.'

'Fucking Ballymena,' one man said scornfully. 'Paisley's country. Well, we have a different way of doing things down here, son, and if you don't like it you don't have to stay.'

'Hang on just a wee minute,' Early said, marshalling his thought hurriedly and cursing his impulsiveness. 'I thought you were interrogating him. What's the use of beating him up so bad he can't talk if you want to ask him questions? That's cutting off your nose to spite your face, so it is.'

There was a pause, during which the salesman mumbled incoherently and his blood formed a small puddle on the tarmac.

'Maybe he has a point, boys,' one man said.

'And look at the blood. Don't get it on you – it's a bastard to get off. When this wee shite goes running to the peelers they'll be looking for bloodstained clothes, so they will.'

The two men holding the semi-conscious salesman immediately released their hold. He fell to the ground like a puppet with the strings cut, and lay there babbling.

'No . . . no trouble. Won't say anything. Won't say a word . . .' Then he passed out.

Early toed him over on to his side. 'Well, he's a lot of bloody use to you now, isn't he? You have to be more subtle about this kind of thing.'

'How would you know?' one man asked, still hostile.

'Sure, you see it on TV all the time. Good cop, bad cop. It's no good just beating the shit out of him.'

Mullan nodded, looking down at the crumpled form on the ground.

'You've a head on your shoulders, so you have, Dominic. Shit, he's a mess, isn't he? Doesn't look as though he'd harm a fly anyway.'

The men shifted uneasily.

'Maybe we should call an ambulance,' said one. 'Do it anonymously.'

'He's a fucking Prod!' another burst out. 'Let the bastard bleed!'

'No,' Early said. 'If you just leave him it'll be the police and the Brits and everything who find him. But if you just call an ambulance, we can keep it quiet.'

He knelt down beside the crumpled body and slapped the face lightly. One bloodshot eye opened.

'You won't say anything, will you, mister? You know what'll happen if you do. We'll find you, and then you'll get worse than a split head, so you will. Do you understand?'

The man nodded numbly through his mask of blood, and Early straightened, satisfied.

'I'll make the call meself. The rest of you might as well clear off.'

They hovered there, indecisive. Early despised them all.

'He's right, lads,' Mullan said. 'You might as well go home. We'll look after this.'

They trailed away, still discontented, muttering. Mullan turned to Early.

'You did the right thing there, Dominic. They've no brains, most of them, just bitterness and biceps, but you're not so slow yourself. Come on, let's see if we can clean the bugger up a bit.'

Charles Boyd slouched in his chair in the operations room at Bessbrook, bored and annoyed. The young Green jacket subaltern who was acting as watchkeeper eyed him a little nervously. This was the gung-ho, fire-eating SAS officer who had led the Drumboy op and wiped out that ASU in Tyrone. So far, all the subaltern himself had had to brave this tour were a few bottles and the insults of the local harridans.

He had three units out on the ground at the moment, two of them on three-day rural patrols under other officers, the third a VCP on the Blaney road, operated in unison with the RUC. All around the room, operational maps of the area lined the walls and at one wall a bank of radios and their operators were an insistent interruption of static and low voices. The young officer sipped his dark brown tea and sighed, thinking of the West End, wondering if someone else was porking his girlfriend while he was away: one of the perennial worries of the soldier.

Boyd's thoughts were more complex. He was trying to think up some way to retrieve what he saw as his reputation. He wanted out on the ground again – he had wanted Gorbals's OP, but Cordwain had overruled him and given it to the Glaswegian NCO instead. The SAS major was in Cross now, overseeing the OP. Boyd was being put on a back burner for a while. He knew it and he didn't like it.

Sometimes he felt that the British Army was not in Northern Ireland to defeat the IRA or to wipe out terrorism, but to maintain a certain status quo. They knew who eighty per cent of the terrorists were, where they lived, what cars they drove, which football team they supported. But they could pin nothing on them. For Boyd that was a ridiculous situation. He believed the terrorists should be taken out – assassinated, for want of a better word. No one in Whitehall would cry for them except for a few tiny special-interest groups and some downright traitors. The judicial system was a farce, and when the army or RUC tried ways of circumventing or speeding it up – such as the use of supergrasses a few years back – then they always failed. Better to see the problem as the IRA saw it – as a purely military one. That would put the shits up the bastards and no mistake. They'd keep their heads well below the parapet after a few of the ringleaders had been found in ditches with bullets in the back of their heads.

But that, Cordwain had told him, would be to become terrorists themselves. Boyd could not see it. There was too much pussyfooting around, and all the while, soldiers and innocents died because of it. Sometimes when he thought about it he could hardly bottle up the fury.

A crackle of the radio. The Greenjacket second lieutenant leaned forward.

'Sir,' the operator said. 'Bravo Two One has stopped a major player on the Blaney road heading east into Cross. Eugene Finn, the name is. He wants to know if you'd like him held for a while.'

'Yes! Keep him there!' Boyd snapped before the other officer could speak. He was out of his chair. 'I want a heli to that VCP at once. We've been looking for this bastard.'

'Have we anything on him?' the Greenjacket asked, looking through his file.

'Nothing concrete – not yet. But it was probably him who masterminded the Drumboy operation. I want to talk to him. Now get me that fucking helicopter.'

The younger officer hesitated, then shrugged, and sent word to the helipad that a chopper was wanted: 'priority two, one passenger'.

It was a small, dragonfly-like gazelle that transported Boyd from the fortress of Bessbrook over the undulating, moonlit hills of Armagh. Ulster Troop was based in Bessbrook because of the fact that it was the best heliport along the border; the SAS needed the mobility it could provide, even though the Security Forces' base in Cross was adequate for most other purposes.

So Finn had come back south. It would be interesting to talk to him, this IRA hotshot. In a way, he and Boyd had already met, over gun barrels. It seemed though that he had survived Drumboy unscathed. A resourceful enemy indeed. The second IRA platoon that had caught them napping that night on the hill – that had been Finn's men, the South Armagh bunch. Intelligence now believed that the South Armagh Brigade had not suffered as badly as they had initially thought. Its members had been spirited away to Belfast. Did this mean that they were beginning to filter back south to their old stamping grounds?

Boyd would get no information out of Finn, he knew that; the man was too canny. And he had nothing to hold him on. Finn's wife, when questioned at her door by chatting British soldiers as to her husband's whereabouts, had merely said that he was away visiting relatives. Nothing to go on, then. But Boyd could at least make this a highly unpleasant evening for the bastard.

The gazelle landed in a field fifty yards from the VCP on the Blaney road. Boyd leapt out. He had no weapon except for the Browning High Power, for form's sake in a webbing holster at his waist instead of in the armpit or on the thigh. He wore a Kevlar helmet and ordinary combats; there was nothing to suggest that he was SAS.

The helicopter took off again. Boyd would stay out and return to Bessbrook with the VCP members themselves. He sauntered over to the road where an old Ford Cortina was sitting to one side and an RUC constable was waving down cars with a red torch.

The corporal in command met him as he gained the road.

'Evening, boss.' The Greenjackets were almost as informal that way as the SAS. 'We've got him out of the car and given him the once-over; we were just going to start and search the vehicle.'

Boyd nodded. 'Go ahead. And Corporal . . .'

The man turned.

'To search it properly, you'll have to take out the seats and things – everything that's remotely movable. You get my meaning?'

The man grinned. 'Sure thing, boss.'

Boyd joined a small group of men in front of the Cortina. There was a soldier there, gripping his SA-80 as though he longed to use it, an RUC constable with his Heckler & Koch MP5K dangling across his armoured chest and his notebook out, and a lean, dark man in civvies who was smoking a cigarette and directing hate-filled glances at them both.

Boyd strode up. 'Evening, Eugene. Nice night for a drive, don't you think?'

Finn looked at him over the glowing tip of his cigarette, and blew out smoke silently.

'Well, constable?' Boyd asked the policeman. The RUC man was young, probably single, as all the police on the border were. He wore an army-style sweater under dark-green Gore-tex waterproofs, and his trousers were bloused into a pair of combat boots. In addition to the Heckler & Koch he carried a Ruger revolver in a holster at his waist. Apart from the green peaked cap with its harp badge, he looked like a soldier.

'Hello, sir,' the constable said cheerfully. Boyd's plummy accent had immediately marked him out as an officer.

'The gentleman here has come from Omagh, where he has been visiting relatives. Name, Eugene Finn, address 23 Conway Crescent, Dundalk Road, Crossmaglen. His driving licence seems to be in order, but unfortunately this is not his vehicle . . .'

'I told you, it's me cousin's,' Finn snarled suddenly.

'. . . and we are checking the ownership now.'

'Thanks, constable. I'll take it from here.'

The policeman nodded and moved away. Finn's eyes darted from Boyd's face to the car that the Greenjacket soldiers were now assiduously taking apart.

'You bastards,' Finn growled as both front seats were taken out and placed in the ditch.

'Now now, sir,' Boyd said with a smile. 'We're just doing our job.'

Finn stared at him closely, then flicked the half-finished cigarette at him so it bounced off Boyd's chest. The SAS officer stiffened.

'That's for your job. Now how long do you think your military sense of humour will keep me here at the side of the road, when me kids are waiting for me at home?'

'Maybe you should spend more time with your kids, Eugene, instead of tramping all over the countryside at all hours of the day and night.'

It was Finn's turn to pause. He regarded Boyd with keener interest.

'What regiment are you with, public schoolboy?'

'Greenjackets, like the rest of them.'

'Is that a fact? You don't carry a rifle. Too heavy for you, is it?'

Boyd felt that he was losing the initiative.

'How are your friends in Belfast, Eugene? Coming along nicely, are they? Poor lads. A punishment shooting is an awful thing.'

'I don't know what you're talking about, Brit.'

'Sure you do, Eugene. Pity we managed to pick up that M60, off the field of battle, you might say. I bet those things don't grow on trees, eh?'

Finn did not reply, but lit another cigarette and blew the smoke into Boyd's face.

'Nasty habit that, Eugene. It'll kill you in the end.'

'Life's a lot more unhealthy for you lot, down here, than it is for me. Maybe Armagh should have a government health warning. "Patrolling here can be bad for your health." How many have you boys lost here in the last eighteen months? It's no wonder you're taking out your frustration on innocent men like me.'

The Greenjackets, eavesdropping on what Finn was saying, went at their work with added savagery. The steering wheel landed in the grass. Finn watched it dispassionately.

'You'll have to put it all back together again, you know.'

'Or what?'

'Or I might have to complain.'

'Who to – the police?'

Finn laughed. 'No – to the Border Fox. Him and his comrades. They're the only real authority in this part of the world. Time you understood that, soldier.'

The corporal joined them.

'Car's clean as a whistle, boss, and we did him before you arrived. Nothing. Omagh confirms that the car belongs to one Jimmy Finn. His story checks out.'

Boyd nodded. 'All right, Corporal. I suppose we had better let Mr Finn be on his way. Pack up the VCP and call in the heli.'

'OK, boss.' The Greenjacket strolled off.

'Going back to hide in your wee base, are you?' Finn sneered. 'I bet it's the only place you feel safe in this part of the world, Brit.'

Boyd smiled, and took Finn's arm in a grip of iron, pulling him closer.

'Listen, Eugene. You can take it from me, not from Parliament, or Whitehall or Lisburn: when we catch this Fox of yours – and we will – he's never going to see the inside of a court. He's going to get the same justice he's been meting out to us for the past eighteen months. That's a promise. And if we catch you stepping out of line, Finn, I swear to Christ, you'll get the same.'

Finn glared at him for a moment and then said: 'You're SAS, aren't you, schoolboy? You were on the hill that night.'

Boyd smiled again, but said nothing.

'Heli's on its way, boss,' the corporal said.

'Very good, Corporal. We'll leave Mr Finn here to his DIY. Have a pleasant evening, sir.' And he touched the brim of his helmet to Finn mockingly. The IRA man stood beside the wreckage of his car and said nothing, but Boyd could feel his eyes on his back all the way across the field where the other soldiers and the policeman were waiting, kneeling in the hedge. It made his skin crawl, as though the cross-hairs of a sight were resting on the back of his neck.

There was a roar, and the helicopter, a troop-carrying Puma, landed, flattening the grass. Boyd was last in the stick, and as he clambered on board he could see Finn still standing motionless in the road, watching them, the glow of his cigarette like a tiny window into hell.

15

Haymaker rubbed his eyes tiredly and peered once more through the powerful magnifying lens of the Nikon. Nothing doing. He stared at the tiny luminous hands of his watch. It was 2330 hours on a Wednesday night, and Lavery's bar was as quiet as a grave. From his position he could see the inside corner of the L-shaped building, covering both the bar itself – though not well, since the windows were frosted glass and the curtains were half drawn – and the private accommodation above and behind it. Gorbals had teased them all, in whispers, with the sight he said he had seen the previous morning. The Lavery woman in the noddy, tits out and ready for inspection. Haymaker thought privately it was a tall tale, designed to make them all look harder. If so, it had worked.

Wilkie was on the radio, his hand on the signals log. He was yawning. God, Haymaker hated OP duty. Lying in wait somewhere, waiting to do the business like they had in Tyrone – that was one thing. But this tedious logging of everyday occurrences was quite another. And if something did happen – if the shit actually hit the fan – then all they would do was inform Cross. And then they would just sit back and watch, like spectators at a football match. So much for the glamorous side of the SAS. He glued his eye to the camera again.

There he was: the undercover bloke, Early. Looked like a bit of a hard character. He was making himself tea in the kitchen. And there was the Lavery woman. Bit of all right, she was; nice hair. Oh, here we go, Haymaker thought, and he squeezed off a few shots of Early kissing her. Lucky bastard.

They went upstairs together, and Haymaker sighed. Wilkie looked at him questioningly and Haymaker made an unmistakable gesture. Wilkie scowled. Being in the SAS was like being a fucking monk sometimes.

Haymaker tensed. There were two cars coming into the square from his right. They were driving slowly, one an old, beaten-up Cortina, the other a Lada. He snapped them quickly, noting their number-plates in the log. One seemed familiar, and he flipped quickly through the P-file. It had been updated that evening. The Cortina – Finn had been driving it on the Blaney road less than two hours before.

Haymaker gave the thumbs down to Wilkie, who nodded. The big trooper squinted down his camera lens as though it were the sight on a weapon – which he often wished it was – and clicked off exposure after exposure. Five men in the two vehicles, all of them getting out at once. He recognized Finn right way: he was the tall, leery bastard smoking the cigarette. Others he found harder to place, but he had their mugs on film, no problem. It looked as though the South Armagh boys were back in town. He entered it all down in the log. They were heading towards Lavery's bar, for a late-night pint or a confab. Or to get Early maybe? Haymaker cursed softly, then showed the log to Wilkie and stabbed a finger at the last entry. Wilkie nodded and began sending the message back to Cordwain in Cross. Haymaker debated waking Gorbals and Raymond, but decided against it. Could be it was all a false alarm, and the other pair badly needed their sleep. No, he'd let them get a little more gonk. The shit hadn't hit the fan yet.

Maggie moaned under him as Early pushed into her. He felt her nails claw his back and her thighs grip his waist. Her face was a pale oval in the darkened room, the hair a shadowed tangle around it.

Then he froze. There were footsteps coming up the stairs, several sets of them.

'Dominic, don't stop. What's wrong?' Maggie whispered.

He rolled off her. 'Somebody's coming.'

'Oh, never worry about Brendan. He doesn't mind now . . .'

'No, not him.'

They were on the landing. Early heard the door of his room being opened, and a voice he recognized.

Finn.

His Walther was behind the cistern, where he always put it when he slept with Maggie. He cursed himself now for his incompetence.

'Get dressed,' he told the naked girl, pulling on his trousers. She stared at him, her eyes shining in the dark.

'It's Eugene. What's he doing here?' she said.

'I don't know. Get dressed.'

She pulled on a dressing-gown hurriedly, just as the door to her room was knocked. Early's eyes met hers, and in that moment he knew that the game was up. She could see his fear.

Without taking her eyes off him, she called out: 'Who is it? I'm in bed.'

137

Early continued to stare at her, talking with his eyes.

'It's Eugene, Maggie. Sorry to bother you. Would Dominic be in there at all?'

She hesitated, her eyes never leaving his face. Then she laughed, bitterly, and said:

'He's here, Eugene. Come on in.'

The door opened, letting in a glare of light. At least three men stood in the doorway.

'Sorry to disturb you, Maggie,' Finn said. He was a shadow, silhouetted by the light behind him. 'We just want a wee word with Dominic here.'

Early straightened. 'Mind if I finish dressing?'

'Oh, go ahead, Dominic. We've all the time in the world.'

Then Finn turned to one of the men behind him. 'Rory, go and get the car started.'

'Going somewhere, are you?' Early asked, lacing up his shoes with trembling hands.

'Oh aye, Dominic. We're all going for a wee ride. You go back to bed, Maggie.'

'I'd like to come along,' she said.

'No, you'll stay here. It's just Dominic we want.'

Early stood up. 'I'm ready if you are, Eugene. Bit late for a drive though, isn't it?'

'Don't you worry – we're not going far. Come on.'

Early paused in his way out of the room to look at Maggie. Her head was bowed, and she did not say goodbye.

'All right, all right,' Early said soothingly as he was shoved along the landing. Brendan stood at the head of the stairs, white-faced.

'What are you going to do to him, Eugene?'

'Nothing, Brendan. Just you shut up the pub as usual after we're gone.'

Early was hustled downstairs, and then out the door. It was cold outside, and under his shirtsleeves his flesh went into goose-pimples. He could still smell the fragrance of Maggie's hair on his skin.

'In you get, Dominic. Mind your head.'

He was pushed into a car, and then shoved down on the floor of the back seat. Finn got in after him and rested his feet on his chest. The IRA man produced a pistol and put it against Early's forehead.

'Now don't you make a sound, Dominic. I'd hate to mess up the floor of me cousin's car, so I would.'

He nodded at the driver, and they moved off. Early shut his eyes, knowing he was a dead man.

Gorbals woke at once to find Haymaker shaking him.

'What? What is it, you big cunt?'

'The undercover bloke, Early. They've taken him.'

The little Glaswegian was immediately alert. 'You've radioed Cross?'

'Yes. They're going to try and intercept them. Two cars, five players. I saw one pistol. If you ask me, our man's fucked.'

Gorbals inched out of his sleeping bag. Even now, they were aware of the need for silence. Their conversation had been in whispers.

'What road did they take?'

'The Monog. They're headed for the border, no doubt about it.'

'Fuck. I hope the QRF catches them before they reach it.'

'Shall we start packing up? Early knows there's an OP in Cross. If they work on him, they'll find out.'

Gorbals nodded. 'Don't pack up the surveillance kit, but get all the rest of the shit put away, ready for immediate evac. And comm Cross for instructions. We'll stay here as long as we can.'

In silence, two of the SAS troopers began packing up their gear and the rubbish they had accumulated over the past few days, while one remained monitoring the radio and the other peered out into the empty streets of Crossmaglen.

After a while the car's motion changed from smooth, fast travel to a slow bump and lurch. With his head down near the floor, Early could feel the vibrations of undergrowth clawing along the underside of the vehicle. Once, when a wheel hit a pothole, his head flew up to jar painfully with the muzzle of Finn's pistol, making the IRA man grin.

They stopped at last and cold air rushed in as the car doors were opened. Early felt vaguely sick from the ride on the floor. He was jerked out by two of his captors and stood, dizzy, trying to collect himself.

They seemed to be in the middle of nowhere. He was standing in tyre-churned mud. The night was still dark though there were stars overhead. Suddenly there was a tiny glow of light, and he could make out the humped shape of a derelict house some yards in front of him. Someone had lit a candle inside.

'Let's go, Dominic,' someone said, and he felt the barrel of a pistol in his back. He recognized the voice: it was Jim Mullan.

'I hadn't figured you out for this sort of caper, Jim,' he said casually over his shoulder.

'You hadn't figured out a lot of things. You're in the shite now, Dominic, if that's your name at all. I hope you're good at singing.'

Early said nothing, but let himself be bundled inside the derelict house. There was a small pool of candlelight there, and several men; and a chair, and rope.

He felt a moment of stark, incapacitating terror, and froze. Mullan pushed him forward again. He shook himself.

'All right, Jim, all right.'

He was going to be tortured. His mind began working furiously. The OP would have seen him being spirited away, so the QRF would have been sent out by now. Probably Cordwain had put the rest of Ulster Troop on alert too. Had they managed to follow him? These men seemed remarkably at ease considering half the border security forces were hot on their tail.

Unless they had made it over the border.

That thought chilled the blood in Early's veins.

'Search him,' Finn said curtly.

Early was shoved up against one damp wall and spreadeagled. Hands ran up and down his limbs, into his pockets. They even examined his shoes.

'Nothing,' Jim Mullan said.

Finn frowned. 'The house is clean too – Maggie checked it.' Then he shrugged. 'We'll soon find out the truth of it anyway. Take a seat, Dominic.' He was smoking a cigarette and smiling, gesturing to the stoutly built wooden chair. Early wanted to kill him, but he had to try to draw this out, to give his own people as long as possible to close in.

'If it's all the same to you, Eugene, I'll stand, thanks.'

Finn nodded to the other men. They advanced and took his arms. Then Finn brought up the pistol barrel.

'Fucking sit down, you cunt.'

Early was propelled to the chair and forced to sit in it. The men started tying his wrists, elbows, knees and ankles to the wood. When they had finished he was bound as rigidly to the chair as though he were part of it. He tried to breathe evenly, to contain his fear. These pieces of shit were not going to see him afraid.

Finn stubbed out his cigarette on the stone wall and lit another.

'Strange things have been happening lately, Dominic, so they have. The SAS are in town. Did you know that? Oh aye. They're in wee Crossmaglen, somewhere, and they have a tout who's doing their dirty work for them. Shocking, isn't it?'

Finn drew in smoke. The other men stirred.

'Work the bugger over now.'

'Fucking turncoat bastard.'

Finn held up his hand.

'We'll try this the easy way first, so we will. We're civilized people, after all.' He knelt down in front of Early.

'Now, Dominic, it looks like you're our number one suspect. You're a man without a past, you know that? You showed up here out of the blue, squirmed your way into Maggie Lavery's bed, and suddenly, you're one of us. Very easy. You're just too good to be true. So what's your real name then, eh?'

'Dominic McAteer. Jesus, Eugene, I don't know where you get your ideas from . . .'

Finn stubbed out his cigarette on Early's cheek.

The SAS officer cried out and twisted his head, but one of the other men grabbed it from behind and held it still. Finn ground out the glowing butt slowly, intently. The smell of burning flesh filled the room. Early clenched his teeth until blood started from the gums.

Finally, Finn straightened. Early's eyes were full of tears. His right cheek felt double its usual size, as though it were swollen with acid. He was breathing like a sprinter.

'You're a hard bastard, Dominic, you know that?' Finn said softly. 'I'll bet my arse you're no navvy from Ballymena. You're a Brit, so you are. Maybe you're even SAS.'

'You're out of your mind, so you are,' Early groaned. He could taste the blood in his mouth.

Finn said nothing, but nodded to the other men, and withdrew.

They began to work on him.

16

Cordwain slammed down the phone savagely.

'They've lost them!'

'How?' Boyd demanded.

'Fuck knows. They must have turned off the Monog road and avoided the VCP near Urcher Lodge. Then they simply disappeared. The checkpoint on the Foxfield road hasn't seen them, and neither has the watch-tower at Drummuckavall. They must have taken off across country.'

'In a car? It's boggy as hell down there.'

Cordwain turned to the operations map on the wall of his office.

'There are dozens of side-roads and tracks down in that area. It could be they went down the Alley road, south-west towards the border, through Moybane, and then turned off into Moybane Bog – there are tracks there, for the forestry workers. They could have taken the car all the way through the woods there, and hey presto! they're in the Republic.'

'Jesus,' Boyd said. 'That's it, then. Early's dead. Poor bastard.'

'They'll keep him alive a while, to try and find out whatever they can. Early's a tough nut. He knows the longer he holds out the more time it gives us.'

'What about the Gardai? Have they been informed?'

'Irish Army units are in the area. They're reacting with their customary lack of urgency. Fuck! What a mess.'

'The troop is ready to go, with the exception of Gorbals's men. They're being extracted now. The rest are all in plain clothes. We have three Q cars standing by in Cross.'

'Good. We're on our own with this one. If they are across the border, then the Regular Army's hands are tied.'

'You'll authorize a cross-border operation, then?'

'Fucking right I will. I'm not going to stand by and let them murder a member of the Regiment under our very noses.'

Cordwain stood staring at the map. Outside, helicopters were roaring as they landed and took off. It was still dark, but the choppers were helping to flood the area south of Crossmaglen with troops. They were more of a gesture than anything else. He was sure now that the enemy was across the border, perhaps only a few hundred metres into the Republic of Ireland, holed up in a house or hut somewhere, torturing Early.

'I want all three Q cars to head down for the Moybane area. That's where they've headed – the VCPs will have funnelled them in that direction. I want one down as far as the footbridge to the east of Moybane Lough, and two covering the forestry area of the bog. You're to continue on foot across the border – it's only two hundred metres away at that point. Sweep the area between the footbridge and the wood. They'll be in an abandoned house, a farmhouse or something.'

'And if we find them?'

'Take them out – as many as you can. And save Early, what's left of him.'

'There'll be an almighty stink – it has the makings of a proper diplomatic incident.'

'I know. I'll take the rap. It was me that got Early into this in the first place. They can have my head on a plate if they like, just so long as we get those fuckers and save our man. Is that clear, Charles?'

Boyd was smiling. 'Perfectly.'

'Then *go*!'

The men in the cars were heavily armed. There were three in each vehicle, one commanded by Boyd, another by Sergeant Hutton, a reliable Falklands veteran, the third by Corporal Little. One man in each car had a Remington 870 pump-action shotgun – useful for blowing hinges off doors. The others carried Heckler & Koch MP5K sub-machine-guns, ugly, snub-nosed little weapons used by SAS hostage-rescue teams. Extra magazines were fastened to the weapons themselves with magnetic clips. As well as these, the men each had their Browning handguns in shoulder holsters and a variety of stun and smoke grenades. The team leaders carried small Landmaster radios with single earphones and wrist mikes.

They were dressed in nondescript civilian clothing: jeans, plaid shirts, bomber jackets. Every man there knew that they were going to undertake an illegal incursion into the Irish Republic, but it was to rescue a fellow soldier.

They were silent in the cars as they sped south, checking magazines, running through room-clearing drills in their heads. They were waved through army checkpoints, who had been told to expect them, and soon they were off the secondary roads and on to single-track roads, and finally unsurfaced tracks.

They split up on a signal from Boyd and headed for the three debussing points, from where they would continue on foot, sweeping a kilometre-wide area for their quarry.

The hunt was on.

A deluge of cold water brought Early round. His head slowly straightened and he tried to blink the droplets out of his eyes. His face was swollen to twice its normal size. It felt as though it belonged to someone else. His mouth felt as though it were full of fine gravel, but that was the remains of his teeth.

He found it hard to breathe, because they had thrust lighted cigarettes up his nostrils until the flesh had charred. He was locked within himself, withdrawn from the world except when the renewal of the agony brought it screaming back into sharp focus.

Two things kept him going, kept his mouth shut and stopped him from telling them everything, from begging for mercy. The first was the knowledge that the SAS would be looking for him. They were probably less than a mile away even now, combing the countryside. Border or no border, he believed that James Cordwain would do his utmost to rescue him.

That's what comes of going to a public school, he thought with dazed humour. A sense of honour. Cordwain will do the right thing, come hell or high water.

The second thing was quite simple. It was white, blinding hatred for the men who were doing this to him, and in particular for their ringleader. Early wanted to survive, because he wanted the satisfaction of killing Finn himself. He wanted to make the IRA man squirm as he was squirming now, wanted to wipe that fucking sneer off his face for eternity.

'Well, Mr X,' Finn said. 'You're no Dominic McAteer from Ballymena, so you're not. You know how I know?'

Early glared at him dumbly.

'Well, it's simple, you see. If you were some humble brickie, you'd be begging for mercy now, promising all sorts of things, and confessing to the murder of your own mother if you thought it would stop the pain for a while. But you're not, not you. You're just sitting there taking it and not saying a thing. Your eyes say it all though.

'You're a Brit, aren't you, me old son?'

Still Early said nothing.

'Well, we'll take that as a yes. Now, Mr X, since we've established that you're a Brit, and a bloody-minded one at that, we want you to talk to us even more. We just can't wait to hear what you have to say, can we, lads?'

There was a snigger from one of the other men. Jim Mullan, Early noted, looked a little green about the gills.

'This freedom fighting is a noble calling, eh Jim?' he managed to croak through his broken teeth. The big man looked away.

Finn slapped Early across his burnt cheek.

'Now now, me old son – no fraternization. You'll answer questions, but I don't want any of your bullshit.'

'Fuck off,' Early rasped.

'Stubborn cunt,' Finn said, not without admiration.

'Rory, go and bring that leather-covered box out of the car. Seamus, what's the time?'

'Just gone two.'

'Ach, sure we've loads of time, so we have.' Finn produced a hip-flask from his pocket and passed it around. The reek of whiskey was strong in the air.

'Want some?' he asked Early, and splashed some over his face.

It burned and seared Early's blistered and raw skin, but he shut his eyes against the pain and made no sound. The hatred mounted up and up in him like a steepening wave.

When he could open his eyes again Early saw that they had brought in a brown box from the car. They opened it and he saw the black, shining shape of a telephone. For a moment he was puzzled, until he realized, and the sweat broke out all over his body.

'You boys used these in Malaya,' Finn said, flicking away another cigarette butt. 'And the Yanks used them in Vietnam. And I'm not talking communications. Seamus, get his trousers down. Get the bastard's balls out.'

Early's trousers were torn down to his knees, then his boxer shorts. Finn came closer, with two crocodile clips attached to wires, and clipped them agonizingly on to Early's testicles.

'Now we'll have some fun,' Finn breathed. 'Your last chance. What regiment are you with?'

Early spat blood and fragments of teeth into his face. Finn straightened.

'Jim, turn that fucking handle.'

Early's world exploded in blinding pain. Involuntarily, he screamed aloud.

Boyd halted, his shoes sinking in the wet ooze of the bog.

'Did you hear that?'

'What, boss?'

'Somebody yelled, I'm sure of it.'

The three SAS men paused in the silent night, hearing an owl kee-wick, the squeak of hunting bats, their own feet sucking in the marsh that they had plunged into as soon as they had crossed the invisible border between Northern Ireland and Eire.

Then they all heard it, carrying over the fields in the silence of the summer night. A man screaming in agony.

'Jesus Christ,' one of the troopers said softly. Boyd felt the hair on his neck rise up. He thumbed the wrist mike.

'Oscar One and Two, this is Zero. Objective to your front, estimate figures three zero zero metres, over.'

'Roger out,' came back the reply from the other two teams.

Boyd lifted a hand, and the three SAS men started forward again.

They were sinking ankle-deep in ooze at every step, their progress frustratingly slow as they hauled their feet out of the sucking mud as quietly as possible. At last one of the troopers tapped Boyd's arm.

'Off on the right, boss – there's a track going our way.'

Boyd nodded and they started towards it. The scream came again, louder now. Boyd felt an urge to run forward, guns blazing, and take out the torturing bastards, but he forced himself to slow down.

They reached the track and made better time. There was a wood ahead, gloomy and impenetrable-looking in the darkness.

Figures moving to their left. Boyd swung the muzzle of the Heckler & Koch.

'They're ours, boss.'

The figures were holding their hands in the air in the recognition signal. Boyd waved them over.

The two teams went to ground in the eaves of the wood, waiting for the third to join them. At last they did, announcing their arrival over the radio before appearing. Sergeant Hutton whispered in Boyd's ear.

'There's a little clearing in the wood ahead, some old derelict building with a light in it. Two doors at the front, one at the back. The screams are coming from there. That's the place, boss.'

Boyd digested this, and then made his plans accordingly.

Two teams would assault the place: his own and Corporal Little's. They would clear the house room by room in two pairs and flush the terrorists out into the open. The third man of each team would remain at the front of the house to provide possible fire support or catch any terrorists who slipped past the room-clearing teams. Sergeant Hutton's troopers would be the cut-off group and would station themselves at the rear of the building to catch any of the enemy leaving that way. There would be no escape for any of them.

The SAS men began moving into position.

17

They had drenched his lower body with water, to strengthen the shocks. Early's head hung over his naked knees. His genitals were scorched and discoloured from the hand-powered generator of the field telephone. There was an unpleasant smell in the air, of ozone and burning hair. He no longer cared. All he wanted was a release from the pain. He would almost have welcomed a bullet in the head, if it meant an end to the pain.

They were not coming for him; there would be no last-minute rescue. Cordwain had abandoned him.

Talk to them, a voice deep inside him urged. Tell them something – anything. Make them stop. It was tempting to believe that if he talked, they would stop. But they would never stop. He was their sport for the evening.

And besides, he thought: I am nothing if not a stubborn sonofabitch.

'Spin her round again, Jim,' Finn said. Even he sounded weary.

'No,' Mullan said. 'Sorry, Eugene. Let one of the other lads do it. I don't feel too well. I need a bit of fresh air.'

Finn stared at him closely, and then laughed.

'Right enough, Jim. You do look as though you're going to puke. Go on, then, go and clear your head. The night's not over yet. We'll have this cunt singing like a bird before dawn.'

Mullan left the room, shambling out into the night air. The other men were standing around, eyes bright, lapping it up.

'Seamus, go and give Jim your gun. Tell him to keep an eye out. And then you can have your turn.'

As the other man went out to do his bidding, Finn knelt in front of Early again.

'You know, Brit, I don't give much for your prospects of being a family man after this little escapade. Your balls are dark as a pair of plums.'

He grinned, but Early was too far gone to care. He could not see Finn's face in any detail – only a white blur.

'What regiment are you?' Finn asked for the thousandth time.

Seamus came in again and knelt beside the field telephone, his hand on the handle.

'Fuck me, Seamus, this bugger's as tight-lipped as a tinker's purse. Spin her again.'

The handle spun round, and it started once more.

Big Jim Mullan stood outside in the welcome fresh air of the night. That stink inside, it had made him sick to his stomach. He didn't like all this interrogation business. If Dominic was a spy, then they might as well shoot him and have done with it. This torturing stuff wasn't his cup of tea at all.

The pistol grip was cold in the palm of his hand. A Beretta Centurion, 9mm – a beautiful weapon. Mullan loved guns, always had, since the time his father had let him fire a shotgun as a boy. Or perhaps since the first time Finn had placed an AK47 in his hand.

He thought of Drumboy. He had been lucky or unlucky to miss that – he wasn't sure which. What a fight. But so many had died, because Dominic had somehow informed, Eugene had said. And that incident with the Prod salesman in Brendan's bar had confirmed Finn's suspicions about Dominic.

Mullan shook his head. Sometimes he wondered if the whole business was worth it at all.

Then he saw the shadows come rushing out of the trees like nightmares made real. The starlight glinted off the barrels of their weapons. He raised his pistol.

'Eugene!' he shrieked. 'They're here!'

A fusillade of bullets blasted him off his feet.

Boyd leapt forward. The big player at the door was on his back, eyes open and his pistol lying unfired at his side. He moved feebly, and Boyd put another two rounds in him – a 'double tap' to the head that blew away half his skull.

Trooper Quigley fired two shotgun blasts into the door of the house and Boyd kicked it off its mangled hinges. Then Quigley swiftly lobbed in a stun grenade. Corporal Little and his partner were at the other door, doing the same.

There was a flash and a bang within, and then Boyd rushed through the doorway.

The blast had blown out the candles. It was dark inside. There was a slumped, seated shape in the centre of the floor, other shapes moving at the back, leaving by a rear door. He opened up on them, the little sub-machine-gun bucking wildly in his hands. There were screams, and someone fell, but the others were still moving. He heard gunfire on the other side of the house as Little's team moved in.

'Room clear!' he shouted, and Quigley burst in. Boyd took a second to check that the figure tied to the chair was indeed

Early, and then joined his partner at the far door. He pulled a pin on another stun grenade and threw it into the next room. After it had gone off, Quigley darted through the doorway, opening up on automatic as he went. Now that they had Early secured they could be less careful with letting off rounds, but they still had to be careful of ricochets. In a house this old and dilapidated there was a lot of bare stone visible that could send bullets bouncing back at their firer.

'Stoppage!' he heard Quigley shout, infuriated. More rounds were going down. He went through the doorway in pursuit and stood over Quigley firing two-round bursts as the trooper changed mags.

'OK!' Quigley yelled, and started firing again himself. Now it was Boyd's turn to change mags.

Another fucking doorway. This one was open, leading out into a kind of back kitchen. There were flashes in the darkness as the players fired back. Boyd was dimly aware that the cut-off team was firing too, out at the back of the house. He and Quigley put down rounds at the flashes and heard someone cry out. Then they moved forward again, as smoothly as a well-oiled machine.

Another stun grenade, then a burst of fire through the doorway. The room was empty but for a body lying in a shining pool at one wall. At the back a broken door was swinging on its hinges and letting in the night air.

'Room clear!' he heard Little shout, and then: 'We're at the back of the house, boss!'

'House clear!' Boyd shouted. There was firing out of the back. The trees were flashing and flickering with gunshots; clearly some of the players had made it to the trees.

A shot behind him. He turned to find that Quigley had put a bullet in the head of one of the downed players.

'Fucker was still wriggling, boss,' Quigley said, and Boyd nodded.

The job was done – there was nothing more for the two assault teams to do for the moment but wait. If they ran out into the woods there would be a danger of a blue-on-blue. Sergeant Hutton was there to see the players didn't escape.

Something moved at the edge of the trees. A man in civvies, crawling into the woods. He still had a pistol in one hand. Boyd put three rounds into him, and he jerked frantically, then lay still.

'I make that four of the fuckers,' he said.

'I think one got away,' Quigley told him. 'He ran out the back with the one you just shot, but I don't think Hutton's lads got him. That's who they're after now.'

'They'd better fucking get him,' Boyd growled, and then: 'I'm going to have a look at our man back there. Keep the backyard covered.'

He strode back through the house, stepping over two bodies on the way. Both of them were well and truly dead, finished off with head shots. Though the operation seemed to have been largely successful, Boyd was uneasy. The SAS were operating on the soil of the Irish Republic; technically, they had just carried out four murders. He wanted his men back in Northern Ireland ASAP, before the Gardai or the Irish Army picked them up.

More shots out the back, then silence. Boyd bent over Early, wincing as he made out what had been done to him. He felt for a neck pulse, got one, and sighed with relief. Then he began slicing through Early's ropes with a pocket knife.

The undercover officer's eyes opened and after a moment his burnt and battered face smiled as he said: 'You took your fucking time.' Then his head fell to one side again.

Quigley came running through the door.

'Boss, Hutton says one of them got away, and there's Southern police cars on their way up the track.'

'Shit! Grab Early. We've got to get the hell out of here.' He thumbed his wrist mike.

'Zero to all stations. Bug out, I repeat, bug out back to debus point, out.'

He and Quigley grabbed the semi-conscious Early's arms and trailed him out to the front of the house. Several other troopers were crouching in the deeper shadow of the trees. Boyd could see two sets of headlights advancing bumpily up the track less than half a mile away.

'Back across the bog,' he told Quigley. They set off. Two more troopers joined them and helped with Early so that each of them had a limb. They made good time until they hit the soft sections of the bog, when they began to sink into the muck up to their calves.

Boyd looked back. Two cars had stopped with their headlights trained on the house, and figures were moving around. It was farcical. Here they were, lugging an unconscious man whose trousers were down around his ankles through a bog in the middle of the night, on the run from the police. And he was a British Army officer on a top-secret mission. Jesus, what a world.

They saw the faint shine of water off to their right. Drummuckavall Lough. They were almost on the border now.

'We bleeding made it,' Quigley gasped. 'Back in the UK, thank fuck.'

When they were sure they were once more back in Northern Ireland they halted a moment while Boyd commed the other team. The troopers had merged into two groups: his four men, and Sergeant Hutton's five.

'Back in from the *ulu*, boss,' Hutton's reply came back. 'All here. One target got away, legged it through the woods. No own casualties.'

Boyd felt suddenly exhausted. The exhilaration of the fire-fight had long since worn off. He was cold, wet and filthy. All he wanted was a bath and a bed.

'Let's get back to the cars,' he said, hauling on Early's arm again. 'We've got a story to get straight.'

Eugene Finn paused, chest heaving, and listened to the night sounds all around him. Nothing but the sound of a nearby stream and his own feet sucking slightly in the mud.

He bent over and grasped his knees. Christ, it had been close. The bastards had nearly caught him in the trees but he had lain under a tangle of brambles for half an hour, still as a stone, until they had all gone. Then he had heard the cars drawing up, and knew it was time to get away.

They were all dead: Jim, Seamus, Rory, Pat. Those SAS bastards had killed every one of them – in the Republic, too. And they had rescued Early. That shite had been SAS himself, all along.

He wondered how Maggie would feel when he told her she had been fucked by an SAS officer. He hoped she'd want revenge.

He straightened again. He was just north of the border, less than two miles from Crossmaglen. It was too dangerous to go back there though; they had been keeping tabs on Early, that much was plain. There must be an OP with a view of Brendan's bar. No, he'd go elsewhere. He had friends all over this part of the world, including one known as the Border Fox.

18

The Commander of Land Forces in Northern Ireland, Brigadier General Brian Whelan, stared at the file on his desk and said nothing. His aide, Major Ben Hastings of the Intelligence Corps, fidgeted uneasily in front of the desk.

'Oh, sit down, Ben, for God's sake,' the CLF said irritably, not looking up.

There was a silence in the office, interrupted only by the sound of Landrovers humming past outside and the clicking of the secretary's keyboards next door.

Whelan straightened at last and produced a briar pipe from a drawer. He filled and lit it, the aromatic smoke making blue threads in the sunlit air of the office.

'I tell you, Ben,' he said absently around the stem of the pipe. 'That's the last time I ever go along with an out-of-channels suggestion. Martin Blair is washing his hands of it, of course.'

'Yes, sir,' the aide said uncertainly.

'So we must carry the can. And what a can of worms it is.' Whelan gestured to the pile of newspapers lying to one side on the desk.

He set down the pipe.

'They will have to go, of course, the whole damned lot of them. We'll ship them back to Hereford. And this Cordwain fellow . . . well, heads will have to roll. The SAS will probably just RTU him, the bloody cowboy. Christ knows we'll have a time of it persuading the Irish Government the raid was without official sanction. This little episode has set back Anglo-Irish relations ten years. It's the last thing the PM needs at the moment.'

'Yes, sir.'

'What about the operative they rescued? Where do we have him at the moment?'

'In Dundonald, sir, strictly subfusc.'

'There's a guard on him I take it?'

'Yes, sir – RUC.'

Whelan barked with laughter. 'They don't trust us to keep an eye on him. What about the families of the dead?'

'They're pressing for a public inquiry. They want the SAS team put in the dock.'

'We can't have that. Our laundry is too dirty to be washed in public at present. I want you to get the Press Liaison Officer on line, get him to make placatory noises, but don't let slip a bloody thing. The situation in Armagh is explosive enough without us admitting to murder.'

'Do you see it as murder, sir?'

'Heck no! I think it was a necessary operation. I'd have done the same thing in Cordwain's shoes.'

When he saw the sceptical look on the aide's face, Whelan laughed.

'All right, so I'd have covered my tracks rather better. This Cordwain fellow seems to be intent on shouldering all the blame. Rather noble of him, if rather naive. And bloody awkward for us. If anyone might end up going into the dock, it'll be him – he ordered the bloody operation. The Irish want his scalp.'

'I see, sir. I'll have the necessary orders issued then – for the removal of the SAS?'

The CLF sucked thoughtfully on his pipe.

'The damned thing is, we need them down there at the moment. Not for any more of this search and destroy stuff, but for surveillance. What feeble intelligence we now have suggests that the PIRA in Armagh – what's left of them – are planning a spectacular by way of revenge. Thanks to Cordwain's man in Cross, and the rest of Ulster Troop, seventeen players in the Armagh or Monaghan Brigades are dead or compromised. That's no mean achievement, despite the political fall-out. And despite the fact that one top-level player got away.' Whelan puffed away in silence for a few moments.

'Blair of 1 RGJ wants them out too. They've been stealing his thunder it seems . . .'

He came to a decision. 'Yes, Ben, issue those orders. Make sure everyone knows they're in the pipeline, and start flying back at least half the Troop. But I want the other half kept in the Province – we need them, blast it. And keep Cordwain here for the moment too – in an advisory capacity. He has a good grasp of the situation down there.'

'If the press finds out you'll be crucified, sir.'

'I know. And I'll have to convince the Secretary of State too. He's hopping mad at being kept in the dark over the whole affair. And the Chief Constable. But I think I can swing it. The Fox is still uncaught. If we can bag him quickly enough then that'll gloss over this episode. The public have a short memory.'

'And the relatives and their inquiry? The Irish will back them?'

'Possibly, but not once we let them know the whole story. I want all the facts filtered through to the NIO, and in turn to the Irish. Christ, were we supposed to stand by while one of our men was tortured to death? And make it clear that every terrorist shot was found to be armed.'

'Yes, sir.'

Whelan stared out of the window, smoking his pipe furiously.

'Rule number one in the army: Cover Your Arse. Well, there are a lot of arses hanging in the wind now – including mine. We'll give the SAS one last chance. If they can take out the Fox – which was their bloody mission to begin with, after all – then we may be able to salvage a little credibility . . .'

Early lay inert under the starched hospital sheets. He was in a private room but if he turned his head he could see the back of the plain-clothes policeman's head through the window in the door.

It was good to know he did not have to look over his shoulder any more. He was back among his own people. But he was burning to know the real details behind the Moybane killings, as the press was calling them. He wanted to know who had died and who had lived.

He touched his testicles gingerly under the sheet. They were almost back to normal size, though still tender. There would in all probability be no permanent damage, the doctors had told him, whereas the scars on his face were there for good, unless he submitted to plastic surgery.

Well, he had always been an ugly bastard anyway.

The door opened, and James Cordwain came into the room, bearing a parcel under one arm. He was in civvies: a nondescript jacket and tie, the Browning making a slight bulge under one armpit.

'Hallo, John,' he said breezily, and took a chair by the bed. 'You look like three pounds of shit that's been squeezed into a two-pound bag.'

Early grinned, making his visitor start.

'Jesus, they didn't leave you much in the way of pearly whites, did they?'

'They're fitting me for crowns or dentures or something, the day after tomorrow,' Early said uncomfortably. He kept forgetting about the sight his shattered teeth must present.

'Well, I've something here that might speed your recovery.'

There was a clink, and Cordwain produced from the bulky parcel a bottle of Scottish malt whisky and two glasses. He twisted off the cap and began pouring.

'Up your arse,' he said, by way of a toast, and the two men savoured the flaming warmth of the Scotch. Early closed his eyes.

'Well, James, tell me what happened.'

Cordwain examined him closely. Early's face looked like one great purple bruise. One eye was still swollen shut and there were ugly burns on cheek and nose.

'How are your balls?' Cordwain asked.

'Still there, still working, just about. Tell me you got Finn, James. Tell me you shot the bastard.'

Cordwain poured them both another drink, darting a quick look over his shoulder at the door. 'You may as well know: we missed him. The bastard got away. The four other players were accounted for though; all South Armagh boys. That's two-thirds of the Brigade out of action now.'

'You missed him.' Early was stunned, disbelieving. 'How the hell did you miss him?'

'We lost him in the trees. We think he must have gone to ground until we bugged out. Anyway, I think even the Armagh boys know when they're licked. Maybe now there'll be some peace down there for a while.'

'You'll have no peace in Armagh while Finn and the Fox are still at large.'

'Perhaps they're one and the same.'

Early shook his head. 'No. I thought that at the start, too, but now I'm sure the Fox is someone else, someone we don't have anything on. He's still out there somewhere, waiting to kill again.'

Cordwain stared into his glass.

'You've seen the papers, I suppose?'

'Which ones? The *Newsletter* is cock-a-hoop. It thinks that the Moybane operation is the sort of thing the British Army should be doing all the time. But the *Irish Times* sees it a little differently.'

'I can imagine. The long and the short of it is that we're in the shit up to our ears. There may be a public inquiry. The Irish Government is going berserk. Four murders on its sovereign soil perpetrated by a bunch of British-trained psychos. Hereford isn't too chuffed either.'

'You're going to get it in the neck, aren't you, James?'

The other man nodded ruefully. 'I'll be RTUd, without a doubt. I'll be named in the inquiry, too. My career is finished, John.'

'When do you leave?'

'That's the odd thing. I know the orders are in the pipeline, and half the Troop – as well as Charles Boyd – are packing up even as we speak. But the other half have been ordered to Cross to await further developments. And I've been ordered to stay put too. It's bloody peculiar.'

'Maybe they have a last piece of dirty work they want you to do.'

'Probably. I'm expendable now, and Blair of 1 RGJ has frozen me out, so I'm almost unemployed down there.'

They were both silent, savouring the Scotch and digesting the news.

'What about you?' Cordwain asked at last with forced cheerfulness.

'Me? Fuck knows. MI5 will want nothing more to do with me after this. I think I'm out of a job, James. We can sign on the dole together.'

'Well, you did a fine job in Armagh.'

'Did I? My brother's murderer is still walking around scot-free, as is the man who tortured me. I've left a lot of scores unsettled . . . Has Finn really disappeared?'

'Yes. And the border is entirely sealed off. We think he's in a safe house somewhere in Armagh, lying low.'

'Well, when he's caught, I can at least testify at his trial. He can't hide for ever.'

Cordwain looked uncomfortable. 'That's something I have to tell you about, John, although you never heard it, not from me or anyone.'

Early looked mystified. 'Go on.'

'Finn will never be brought to trial. I've heard from Rumour Control that the NIO will back off in Armagh in return for the Irish Government's co-operation in playing down the Moybane affair. The relatives may push for an inquiry, but the South won't back them up.'

'And in return, the army turns down the heat in Armagh,' Early said in a cold, bitter voice.

'Yes, So you see, Finn is to be left alone, at least for a few months, until this furore dies down.'

'Politics,' Early said, disgusted beyond measure. 'Jesus fucking Christ.'

'It may also be why I'm still here,' Cordwain said blackly. 'I'm being held in case they need to sacrifice me to grease the political wheels.'

Early stared into his empty glass.

'I'm going back in, James.'

'What?'

'I'm going back down there. I don't care if I serve twenty years, but I'm going to find Finn and the Fox and I'm going to kill them both.'

'You're in no condition to do anything.'

'Give me a few days, and I'll be out of here. Nobody knows what the hell to do with me. I'll slip through the official net, no problem.'

'John, don't be a fool.'

'Finn is hanging around the Cross somewhere. I'll need a Q car, and a weapon, of course. My Walther is behind the toilet in Lavery's bar.'

'You really think you can find him?'

'You forget that I lived in that community for a while. I've heard names mentioned. Finn will be in a safe house, the house of a sympathizer, and I know most of the candidates for his landlord. It shouldn't be too hard to figure out which of those locations he's staying at.'

'You're a dead man if you go anywhere near Cross, John. They know who you are, for God's sake.'

Early smiled his hideous smile.

'But not who you are.'

19

The car, an ageing Ford Escort, was parked in Slieve Gullion forest, nine kilometres east of Crossmaglen and a mere two north of the border. The two men inside it were dressed in sturdy hiking boots, cotton trousers and civilian waterproof jackets over thick shirts. One was studying a map, the other was looking intently at a piece of paper.

The evening was drawing in, and the woods around them were silent. They had driven off the Glendesha Road and bumped the car up through meandering forestry tracks for what seemed like miles, before finally parking the vehicle in the shadow of the pines and spruces of the plantation. The tracks had been wiped away, and all over the bonnet and roof of the car were laid old grey blankets, overlaid with a tangle of branches and foliage. The blankets cut out shine and disguised shape, the branches adding to the effect. The men in the car did not want a passing army helicopter to notice anything odd in the wood; they were only three kilometres from Forkhill Security Forces base, on the other side of Croslieve Mountain.

'There's quite a few names on this list,' Cordwain said doubtfully. 'You believe we can check them all out?'

Early shrugged. 'If we have to. But I'm hoping that I may be able to pick up info of one sort or another along the way – tonight especially.'

'And I see that Lavery's bar is down here. John, you can't seriously believe that Finn would go back there?'

'Why not? The place has been raided since Moybane, and found to be clean. He might think it's the last place we'd look – under our very noses. And besides, the twats in the search team weren't told to look for my Walther. It might still be where I left it – I want it back.'

'Christ,' Cordwain said. 'I must be out of my fucking mind.'

'Or out of options. We're both finished with the Regiment, James. You want to go out with a bang as much as I do.'

'But not with a court martial.'

'You've done nothing wrong. Nobody said you could no longer sign out weapons or a Q car. They're all too busy ignoring you to worry about what you might be up to.' Early laughed sourly.

Cordwain tucked away Early's list.

'First one tonight, then – Brian McMullan, Oliver Plunkett Park; less than two miles away. What's the route in?'

The pair of them pored over the map, agreeing on a route to the objective. They had driven past it earlier in the day; the last house in a row of semis in a small, isolated estate. There was a stream running along the front of the houses within a deep, overgrown ditch – that was their approach route.

Cordwain had signed out two Browning pistols and a pair of Heckler & Koch MP5Ks: sub-machine-guns small enough to be hung unobtrusively below one armpit. The Brownings they simply carried in the pockets of their waterproofs. They each had also a small day-sack with odds and ends of food, waterbottles, red-light torches and a small radio that could pick up army and police frequencies; they had no wish to run into a foot patrol.

Once it was fully dark they set off on foot across the fields and streams, and along the back roads, of South Armagh. Their presence was unsuspected by both the locals and the Green Army; Cordwain had logged in a false route and false timings with Operations. According to them he was up in Belfast, preparing his Freds for his imminent departure. It was another reason they could not afford to be stopped by a VCP.

Swiftly and silently, the two SAS men made their way to their objective, the last two hundred metres of the route being in the stream that fronted the house and its neighbours. They were soaked and scratched, and surprised skipping water-rats in the dark, but no observer could have marked their passing.

Early stopped. The gurgle of the knee-deep stream covered what noise they were making and the brambles concealed them as effectively as a curtain. A good position with regard to concealment, but crap for defence.

'We're here,' he whispered to Cordwain.

They leaned into the vegetation-choked bank and slipped out their surveillance gear. A pair of Night Vision Goggles, a small but powerful pair of infrared binos, and the Nikon.

Early stared through the NVGs intently. Nothing doing. Everyone was in bed, as they should be. No dogs, either, which was a bonus.

'All clear,' he whispered to Cordwain, and after the other officer had given him the thumbs up, he slithered off.

Brian McMullan, Sinn Fein activist, interned 1972, in 1974 jailed for seven years for possession of arms. Now a middle-aged family man with three daughters. He had worked at the same site as Early, or Dominic McAteer as he had been, and he had been drinking buddies with Eugene Finn and Dermot McLaughlin, the quartermaster. He topped Early's list of candidates for owners of safe houses. McMullan had kept his nose clean for eight years and was considered a dead letter by the Security Forces.

He was not especially bright, and had been merely an IRA foot-soldier, but he was revered as such by many of the young men of the area. They did not know perhaps how polite he was to the Security Forces when they stopped his car or patrolled through his back garden. His house had not been searched since the late seventies; it was a fairly safe bet for Finn.

Early crossed the road in a rush, the Heckler & Koch slapping the side of his ribs as he made it into the impenetrable shadow of a ditch on the far side. He twisted the dial on the NVGs until they were pouring out an invisible beam of infrared light and the night was clear as noon. Then he moved round to the back of the McMullan house.

No alarms, nothing. They were trusting people, these country folk, when they weren't murdering soldiers.

He plucked a handful of grass from the hedge at the back and wiped his boots with it meticulously. Then he pulled on a pair of surgical gloves and moved up to the house.

He flicked out his lock-pick and began fiddling at the back door, looking round constantly. Thank God there was no moon.

There was a click. He inched back the last of the tumblers in the lock, felt them snick into place, and smiled. An SAS corporal had taught him how to do that years ago.

A small creak as he opened the door. He was in the kitchen. He paused, noting windows, doors, locks, and then unholstered the Heckler & Koch. It was already cocked. He held the stubby weapon in one hand and began checking the downstairs rooms one by one.

Empty. He began moving up the stairs step by step, the little SMG held out in front of him, the goggles covering the whole top of his face, making him look like a bug-eyed creature from another planet.

He would have preferred to move through the house without the NVGs and the weapon; then if he was discovered he might be mistaken for a common burglar. But if he did run into Finn, he wanted to be sure of his man.

He paused at the top of the stairs, turning things over in his head. He could hear quiet snoring from one bedroom. Four doors, two for the kids, one for the parents, one bathroom. He looked at the ceiling. No roof space, it seemed; no entry that he could see, anyway.

He checked, room by room.

Two little girls lying curled up in the same bed, teddies on their pillows. One girl alone, an adolescent with one forearm thrown above her head. And good old Brian and the missus. It was she who was snoring.

Early paused, checking the floor for snags, then he padded into the room. He would leave a trail of drips behind him from the stream but he hoped they would be dry by morning.

He thought for a second, staring down at the sleeping couple. Cordwain was right. The checking-off of his list was too vague. He needed concrete intelligence as to Finn's whereabouts. Perhaps the plan needed to be altered a little.

He bent down beside the bed and placed one gloved hand over McMullan's mouth at the same time as he gently touched the man's temple with the cold muzzle of the SMG.

The eyes opened, then widened. Early felt the man's mouth move under his hand and clamped down tighter. He pushed the weapon's muzzle into the corner of Mullan's eye and then spoke in a whisper, putting on the harsh, guttural accent of the Belfast ghetto.

'Not a word, Brian. Not a fucking sound. All right?'

McMullan nodded, terrified, and Early withdrew his hand but kept the gun pointed at his head.

'Don't you be worrying. The boys just want a wee word. Downstairs. Now.'

He backed away and McMullan clambered out of bed. His wife hitched up an octave higher in her snoring, turned over and then was still again. Poor bastard, Early found himself thinking, sleeping next to her every night.

He made McMullan precede him down the stairs, with the MP5K touching his back all the way. They both entered the kitchen at the bottom and Early stopped him from switching on the light, then gestured to a chair. The man huddled there in his pyjamas, shivering, obviously terrified.

'Don't worry, Brian,' Early said soothingly. 'You haven't done a thing. You don't know me, but I'm not from this part of the world. I'm with the boys up in the city.' He lowered the gun and stretched out a hand. 'We know you've done your bit for the cause in your time, so we do.'

McMullan shook the gloved hand gingerly. 'What do you want then?' he asked hoarsely.

'I'm here to warn you, so I am. We've word that the Brits are for searching this house tomorrow night, or maybe the night after. They're looking for Eugene, so they are; the bastards are turning over every stone in Armagh looking for him.'

'But he's not here,' McMullan protested.

'Ach, we know that, but we like to be sure of these things, you know, and we thought you'd like a wee warning, so you could get the kids out of the way and the china packed and suchlike.'

'Well . . . aye. Thanks, that's good of you. But what's a Belfast Volunteer doing down here?'

'Trying to get Eugene Finn the hell out of here and up to the city again in one piece. You know he was up there before, after Drumboy; well now – I can talk to you about these things, Brian, seeing as you're an ex-Volunteer yourself – now the Army Council have decided it's far too fucking risky for him to stay in Armagh. They have a place ready for him up in the city again. I have to get the bugger out of here in one piece.'

Early paused, waiting. He did not want to have to come out and ask McMullan where Finn was, but he would if he had to.

'What's that you're wearing on your head?'

'Night Vision Goggles. Good, aren't they? Like something out of *Star Wars*, so they are. We got them from America. Now Brian, about Eugene.'

'He's fucking mad,' Brian said, shaking his head. 'He's a fucking lunatic. You're going to have a hell of a time getting him out of there. Right under their bloody noses. I tell ye, I think he's been too smart for his own good this time.'

'Have you seen him since that Moybane thing, then?'

'Seen him? I was out drinking with him last night.'

Early was startled into silence.

'All he can think about is revenge. It's a good job you boys are here to get him out to the city. He needs to get out of Armagh, like you said. And poor old Brendan Lavery – he's at his wits' end. He's not what you'd call a hard-core activist, you know. It's his sister. Now there's a marvellous woman.'

Early held up a hand. 'Brian, I must be on me way, or the boys'll be getting nervous. I hope those bastards don't

175

make too big a mess of the house, and I'm sorry if I scared you there.'

McMullan waved a hand. 'That's all right, so it is. Just you keep up the struggle, and say hello to Eugene for me.'

'Oh, I will,' said Early, and he slipped out the back door, into the moonless night.

'The cheeky bastard,' Cordwain said, shaking his head. He took a slug from the hip-flask and passed it to Early.

'Yes. Obviously, he's intent on staying – and on stirring up more mischief. So there he is, sitting maybe three hundred metres from Cross Security Forces base, drinking with the locals.'

'Balls of brass,' Cordwain said, then looked apologetically at Early.

They were back in the car, muddy and wet from their two trips across the fields. On the way back they had had to shelter in a ditch for a quarter of an hour while an army Gazelle with a searchlight ranged back and forth across the countryside like a wolf on the prowl. The forest had been as dark as pitch when they returned, and even Early had had some difficulty in locating the vehicle once again.

'We can't just go tearing into Lavery's bar with guns blazing,' Cordwain said. 'And what about McMullan? You told him his house would be raided within the next day or two. When that doesn't happen, he's going to start getting suspicious. I know he's not the smartest bloke in the world, but even he will have enough sense to warn Finn there's something in the air.'

'Never worry about it,' Early said imperturbably. 'McMullan's house will be raided all right – you'll see. Now it's time to get a bit of kip. The first stag is yours, James. Wake me up in a couple of hours.'

He reclined the passenger seat of the car, fished out a lightweight sleeping bag, and was soon asleep with his mouth open, his newly capped teeth gleaming slightly in the dark.

Cordwain cursed silently, then got out of the car and stood listening to the night noises. He looked at his watch. It was two-thirty. Another two hours until dawn.

He was uneasy. Though he had been known as a bit of a cowboy in his time, he had never gone so far off the rails before. Admittedly, the Moybane incursion had been a large black mark, but he knew that to all the lower and middle-ranking members of the SAS it had been a success. It was the upper echelons who were about to ruin him for it. He felt very bitter.

Early obviously did not care one jot for the consequences of his actions. He was as set on revenge as that bastard Eugene Finn was. The two were more similar than either of them might like to think; a couple of loose cannons.

So what was he doing here? He found it hard to answer his own question. Seeking some kind of justice perhaps, no matter how rough it might be. Or perhaps he was just getting even, like Early. Too many people had died to let the thing unravel now, just because some pen-pushers in Whitehall or Dublin said so. No, he was here to finish the job properly, to tie up the loose ends. And deep down he believed that if he and Early came up with the goods – if they could somehow take out both Finn and the Fox – then despite officialdom, they might somehow escape the heavy hand of disciplinary action. The waters in Northern Ireland were murky at the best of times, but at the moment they were damned-near opaque. It would be easy for the Regiment, or indeed the CLF to shield himself and Early one way or another.

But there was the rub: they had to come up with the goods. Finn they could manage, perhaps, but Cordwain still could see no clear way of nailing the Fox. He thought that Early might be concocting a way though, and he was not sure if he liked it.

They moved out just before sunrise, easing the car out of the forest and on to the deserted roads. They stopped at an isolated phone box at Early's insistence, and he made a long call without putting any money into the slot. When he got back into the car he was grinning broadly.

'Who was that, your mum?' Cordwain asked him as they moved off again.

'Better than that, my old son,' said Early. 'That was the Confidential Telephone. I've just been telling it that Finn is staying in the McMullan house – anonymously, of course. If the Greenjackets don't raid it in the next day or two then I'm an Irishman.' He laughed.

'So you've gained us time,' Cordwain said, refusing to share his high spirits. 'What now? Do we go after Finn?'

'Not just yet. I want to have a look at the place and do some thinking.'

'What are you going to do – walk in there and have a pint?'

'No, James, I'm not. You are.'

Lavery's bar was quiet as Cordwain walked in. A couple of old men were sitting in the corners reading the *Irish Times* and sipping pints of porter. Brendan Lavery was behind the bar, bottling up. He looked thinner, Cordwain thought, and tired. All the excitement must be getting to him.

'What can I do you for?' the care-worn landlord asked Cordwain, straightening with a grimace.

'Pint of Guinness, thanks. That's a fair day, so it is.'

Lavery looked out the sunlit windows as the black beer came trickling into a pint glass. 'Aye, it's not bad.' He was regarding

Cordwain closely, and the SAS officer wondered if he could remember him from his last, brief visit to the pub. He hoped not, though it shouldn't make much difference if he did.

Taking out his own copy of the *Irish Times*, Cordwain retired to a corner table, nodding at the old men who watched him over the top of their papers. He felt as though everyone was on edge, and had a momentary urge to get the hell out of there. He forced himself to sit down, however, and shake out his newspaper. His job, Early had told him, was to act like a sponge, to notice everyone who came in and out, but to remain aloof.

Cordwain disliked taking orders, especially from someone who was nominally his subordinate, but Early was the one with all the ideas at the moment, so he had no choice. The other SAS officer was currently checking out the derelict houses at the other end of the square where Gorbals's team had had the OP. Why, he would not say, to Cordwain's immense irritation. He felt that Early was treating all this as some sort of game, and he didn't like it.

People came and went throughout the early afternoon. There was no sign of the Lavery woman, or of Finn, though that was hardly surprising. But there was a tenseness about the atmosphere in the bar and especially about the landlord, that was intriguing.

The afternoon drew on, and the men of Lavery's Construction came in after work, raising the noise level. Cordwain clocked their faces one by one, but could identify none as local players. He glanced at his watch and decided to give it another thirty minutes. If he sat there on his own for much longer he would begin to excite comment.

Then he hit paydirt. The Lavery woman came in, and with her was Patrick Mooney, a known player who was one of the few survivors of Drumboy. As they talked to Brendan at the bar Cordwain finished his pint and left the empty glass on the counter, his ears pricked. He folded his paper nonchalantly, and watched the two go behind the bar and through the door that led upstairs. The Lavery woman had been talking about the dinner. It looked as though Mooney was staying in the pub at the moment as well as Finn – perhaps as extra muscle. Cordwain turned and left.

'So you didn't see Finn,' Early said, wiping the Heckler & Koch with an oily cloth.

'Not a whisper. It looks like we'll have to take Mooney into account though. He's a youngster, but a vicious little bastard. He's probably there as a dicker of sorts, or maybe he's to provide a distraction if the army swoop on the place. I'll bet my bollocks there's a small arsenal concealed in that pub somewhere – as well as your bloody Walther.'

'As well as my bloody Walther,' Early echoed soberly.

'So what's the plan, and why were you sniffing round those derelict houses to the north of the square?'

Early cocked and recocked the little SMG several times; then, satisfied, he set it down and took up the magazine, and began unloading it. The snub-nosed 9mm bullets fell into his lap as he eased them out one after the other. When the mag was empty he oiled it and tested the spring. Satisfied, he began reloading it again.

They had parked the car in yet another wood, this one near Silverbridge, some seven kilometres from Cross. The afternoon was waning, the sun going down behind the hills to the west, and Cordwain was restless. They were wasting time, he thought. The McMullan thing would not fool the local players for long. Soon they would contact the men in Belfast and put two and two together.

'The plan,' Early said at last. 'You'll love it. It involves tying up a lady.'

'The Lavery woman.'

'Maggie, yes. There are a few rolls of parcel tape in the back, as well as a couple of Balaclavas. We want to make this look as unmilitary an operation as possible.'

'Shouldn't be difficult,' Cordwain muttered.

'We incapacitate Mooney and the Laverys and spirit our friend Eugene away to a convenient location.'

'Where?'

'Under everybody's noses. I was checking out a few places around Cross today – discreetly, of course. The derelict houses in the square are too near to inhabited buildings, otherwise they'd be ideal. But there's a disused sewage works just on the outskirts, off the Dundalk road, and screened by trees, that's perfect. Very fitting, don't you think – a sewage works?'

'It's too close,' Cordwain said.

'No. Because as soon as we have the Fox's identity from Finn, we move in again. I'm sure the Fox is in Cross itself, so we don't want to have to drive over half the country to get him. This way, it'll be more of a lightning strike. It'll all be over by morning.'

'How do we persuade Finn?'

Early smiled evilly. 'The same way he tried to persuade me – only this time there will be no SAS riding to the rescue.'

'You mean kill him, of course, not hand him over to the RUC or the army.'

'Yes. Once we have the Fox as well we'll dump both of the bodies in the Republic. Eugene Finn will remain disappeared for good. If we handle it right, then we may be able to pass it off as an internal feud – the locals already think that the Belfast boys are in town. And I'm sure your Freds up there will be willing to give us alibis if we need them. No one will know what really happened.'

Cordwain thought it over. It seemed a harebrained plan, but he had to admire its pure brazenness.

'All right,' he said at last. 'When do we move in?'

'Tomorrow night.'

20

Finn flicked the cigarette butt away and drew out another. It was always cold down here, always damp. He was sick and tired of it. Tomorrow night he'd have another few pints in the bar after hours, to celebrate.

He was sitting on a pile of blankets and an old sleeping bag in the cellar of Brendan Lavery's bar. The air was heavy with the yeasty smell of beer and the sour reek of his cigarettes. Moisture ran down the walls. What a fucking dump. He lit his next cigarette, drawing the dry, sweet smoke deep into his lungs. Thank Christ for fags. They kept him going.

He only had himself to blame. He could have been across the border by now, living it up in Dublin, or drinking in some wee shebeen out in the Donegal mountains. But he had chosen to stay.

Finn lifted up the 9mm Walther pistol and studied it with narrowed eyes. He wiped some grit off the gleaming barrel, and smiled. Dominic had left his toy behind the cistern. What a shame. And two spare mags, too. Why, it was just like an early Christmas, so it was.

He stripped the weapon, familiarizing himself with it once again. It had been a windfall, finding that Brit's gun, since so many weapons had been lost at both Drumboy and Moybane. Fuck, but things had really messed up lately. Belfast would not be pleased, not at all. He would have some fast talking to do if he was to stay on here as ASU commander, and try to build up what was left of the Brigade again.

That Brit, McAteer, or whatever his real name was – it was all his fault. If it hadn't been for him neither of the two disasters which had struck the Volunteers in Armagh would have happened. God knows where those SAS bastards had spirited him away to. He was probably in England now, being treated like a hero. Maggie had been a bit strange after all that. She had wanted to know exactly what Finn had done to McAteer before the Brits showed up. If Finn hadn't known any better he would have said she was concerned for him, the cunt.

All that was past them now. He had to lie low while he planned this next strike – something to get the Brits running around like headless chickens, like they had been before Drumboy.

The papers were full of stories about how the SAS were being withdrawn from Ireland in the wake of the border incursion that had resulted in the deaths of four men. At least that was one good thing among all the bad. Maybe now things might return to normal. Or as normal as they ever were in this part of the world.

He threw aside part of the heap of blankets to disclose a bundle of wires and a digital clock-face; also a bulky package wrapped in greaseproof paper. Finn smiled again. It was a long time since he'd set up one of these fuckers. It would be good to get his hand in again. And Maggie, she would help him. She was a hell of a woman.

He'd slept with her once, back just after her husband had died, and that had been a night of fireworks, lingering in the memory.

He got to his feet, cigarette dangling from his mouth, and stepped deeper into the far corner of the cellar. Behind the beer-kegs was a blanket-shrouded shape. He drew off the covering and gazed at what was underneath with his eyes shining. They'd have to move everything, of course, before fresh deliveries were made down here on Thursday, but for the moment, he was looking down at a thing unique in Ireland: a Barratt-Browning .50-calibre rifle: the weapon of the Border Fox.

The SAS were going to get a going-away present.

For Charles Boyd, the past few days had been a hectic nightmare. It was midday on the day the first half of Ulster Troop was being hustled out of the Province, and though he had not been in the field since the Moybane operation, he was as exhausted as if he had just been out on rural patrol.

The twelve men who were leaving included Haymaker, Raymond and Wilkins. Gorbals McFee would be staying behind with the rest, though Rumour Control had it that they might be on their way out soon after. Cordwain, Boyd had not seen in three days. He was up in Belfast, tying up loose ends. And Early – he had checked himself out of Dundonald Hospital and then disappeared. Boyd had never liked him anyway, but he couldn't help wondering where Early was, and if Cordwain was somehow involved.

Anyway, it was not his problem any more. His kit was packed, and both he and the half-troop were ready to board the Puma helicopter that was waiting on the helipad to fly them to RAF Aldergrove, near Antrim. From there they would be put on a plane to Brize Norton, and his dealings with Northern Ireland would be over. He had mixed feelings about the whole thing. Glad though he was to be going away, he knew that he and the men were being shuttled out in disgrace, scapegoats for the politicians in the wake of the Moybane operation. And there was also the unfinished business they had left behind them: Finn and the Fox still at large.

Haymaker came through the open door and jerked a thumb back up the corridor.

'The Crabs are ready when you are, boss; they're warming up the heli now. They want us on the pad in figures ten.'

Boyd waved a hand, and Haymaker left again.

He looked around him at the cramped little room he and Cordwain had shared. He would not miss it. Then he shouldered his kit and exited without a backward glance.

The Puma was roaring on the tarmac and the SAS troopers formed two sticks pointing towards its cockpit in an inverted V. At last the pilot gave the thumbs up, and they ran forward at a crouch, weapons in one hand, bergens in the other. Their equipment, including the weapons, would go back with them to Hereford.

They scrambled on board the helicopter, swearing loudly at one another as they packed the interior space as tightly as a sardine tin. Boyd boarded last, and tapped the pilot on the shoulder. The Puma rose slowly; it was carrying almost maximum load. He looked out through the doorway and saw the helipad recede, then shut the side door.

'Goodbye, fucking Armagh,' he said.

The Puma banked and began the turn that would take it up over the hills surrounding Bessbrook. Boyd looked back down the crowded interior of the helicopter. The men were seated on the flimsy canvas seats, their bergens on their knees, the muzzles of their weapons kept well away from the fuselage.

There was a sudden ticking noise that could be heard even over the roar of the engine. It was like someone punching a hammer on a sheet of tin. Boyd was about to ask the pilot about it when the Puma lurched crazily and he was thrown across the interior like a sack of potatoes. The crew were shouting to each other.

'What the fuck?' someone yelled.

The helicopter suddenly dropped. Boyd felt his stomach lift with the sudden descent. He laboured over to the pilot's shoulder.

'What's going on?' he shouted.

'We're taking ground fire. They've hit the tail rotor. I'll have to put her down. Get your men to brace themselves!'

'Jesus Christ.' Boyd turned to the tightly packed SAS troopers.

'Crash positions! We're going down!'

At that moment a hole the size of his fist appeared in the fuselage. There was a smell of burning, and of spilled fuel. The Puma swooped and the SAS men hung on to whatever they could find. The bergens and weapons went flying around, and a loose rifle struck Boyd, laying open his forehead.

'We're going to hit!' the co-pilot yelled. 'Brace yourselves!'

There was an enormous impact, and then an explosion of flame.

Twenty seconds after the crash, the first mobiles were powering out of Bessbrook. A Lynx gunship with medics and a four-man brick was first on the scene, and the Landrovers of the mobiles roared along the quiet, sunlit country roads with more troops to cordon off the area.

The lead Landrover of the first mobile was passing over an old stone culvert when the bomb went off. It blew the vehicle off the road, crumpling in one armoured side as though it were cardboard. Lumps of stone from the shattered culvert were blown through the air like shrapnel, hitting the second Landrover and smashing its bulletproof windscreen. The second vehicle swerved to a halt. Soldiers poured out of the rear two vehicles and ran across the field to where the remains of the first Landrover were lying. The culvert was now a smoking crater. Bodies lay mangled in the grass. Someone was moaning. The soldiers knelt among the dead and dying and began to administer first aid while the report went back to Bessbrook that they had been ambushed.

Early was filling up at the petrol pump when Cordwain came walking back out of the little service station, white-faced, and got behind the wheel of the car without a word. Early settled the bill and then they pulled out. It was not until they had driven almost a mile in silence that Cordwain spoke.

'There was a television in there; I just caught the news. There's been a helicopter shot down just outside Bessbrook, fourteen on board. No word yet on a final casualty figure, but there are at least three dead.'

Early said nothing, and Cordwain went on.

'That was Ulster Troop. They were to fly out today at noon. Charles Boyd and eleven of my men were in that heli.'

'What shot them down?' Early asked harshly.

'They're not sure yet, but it looks like something heavy, using armour-piercing rounds. That's all they know.'

'The Fox,' Early said flatly.

'Yes. But that's not all of it, John. Bessbrook is short of choppers at the moment. That's why the troop went out in a Puma instead of in a Chinook. So most of the troops sent out after the crash were in 'rovers. They were ambushed. A culvert bomb. Again, they haven't reached a final figure yet, but it looks like no one in the lead vehicle survived.

Early hung his head. Most Landrovers carried three to five men.

'How was it detonated?' he asked.

'No idea – it's just come up on the news. Probably a command wire.'

'Finn,' Early said softly.

'Yes. Finn and the Fox. You were right, you know. There will be no peace in this part of the world until they're both dead.'

'Does this mean that Finn may no longer be based in Lavery's, I wonder?' Early mused.

'Maybe. But we're going in tonight, as planned. It'll be my last chance – they'll want me down in Bessbrook to help sort out the mess. I must go back tomorrow.'

'Tonight, then,' Early agreed. 'Tonight we take out both of them, one way or another.'

'Yes. You see, John, it's personal for me now, as well as you. I don't care if I do twenty years, but tonight we're going to even the score.'

21

'It's quiet tonight,' Maggie said, cleaning a glass with rapid twists of the cloth in her hand.

'Aye,' Brendan said. He was leaning against the bar reading the paper with a half-full tumbler of whiskey in front of him.

'Where's that Mooney fella?' he asked his sister.

'Out the back, keeping an eye out.'

'And Eugene?'

'In the cellar, same as always. He wants to come out for a drink or two this evening.'

Brendan sipped at his whiskey. He looked as though he had sipped a lot of whiskey lately.

'Where'd you get to this morning anyway?'

'I told you, I went for a drive.'

He shook his head. 'That was desperate today, all those deaths. Jesus, Maggie, what a country.'

Maggie began cleaning a second glass, holding it up to the light to check for imperfections.

'Sure, they were all Brits, so they were – SAS most of them. They got what they deserved.'

'I'm sick of it, Maggie, sick of it all. I want Eugene out of here.'

'He won't be here much longer,' she said soothingly.

'It was him planted that bomb, wasn't it? I saw him come back in this afternoon, Mooney driving the car with a grin on his face as wide as a banana, the pair of them covered with muck. It was them did it, didn't they?'

Maggie laid a finger against her brother's lips. 'What you don't know can't harm you. Don't think about it, Brendan.'

'Don't think about it! Jesus, Mary and Joseph.'

'Turn on the news, there's a good fella. I want to hear what's going on.'

Brendan pressed the remote listlessly and the TV above the bar flicked into life. *Good Evening Ulster* had just started.

'There were two attacks today on the Security Forces in South Armagh. The first was on a helicopter which army sources say was transporting troops to RAF Aldergrove . . .'

Eugene Finn and Patrick Mooney entered the bar through the interior door and wordlessly pulled themselves pints of Bass. Mooney winked at Brendan and Finn looked at Maggie. Then they sat and watched the news like children mesmerized by a Christmas tree.

'The helicopter was hit by heavy-calibre gunfire from the ground and was forced to make an emergency landing near its base. Eyewitnesses state that the aircraft was in flames as it descended and that it blew up as it hit the ground. Army sources have confirmed that three of the occupants were killed, one of whom is believed to be the pilot. At least eight others were seriously injured.'

Moony cheered and slapped hands with Finn. Maggie watched the news impassively.

> '*Army sources refuse to comment on press speculation that the attack was the work of the so-called "Border Fox", who for eighteen months has been carrying out attacks on both the police and the army using a high-calibre weapon. They also declined to confirm rumours that the Puma helicopter was carrying SAS soldiers when it was shot down.*
>
> '*Minutes after the first, a second attack was then carried out on army vehicles which went to the aid of the downed helicopter. It is believed a bomb was planted by a command wire when the lead army Landrover passed over it. All four occupants of the vehicle were killed, three of them dying at the scene, the fourth on the way to hospital. The army have yet to release their names but it is thought they were members of the 1st Battalion the Royal Greenjackets, who are stationed in the area.*'

Finn and Mooney clinked glasses, beaming.

'Will you not join us, Maggie?' they chorused. 'Seven of the bastards in one day. It's another Warrenpoint, so it is.'

Maggie poured herself a brandy and sipped it calmly.

'Brendan, you go upstairs and have a lie-down – you don't look so well, so you don't. I'll look after the bar.'

Her brother left without protest. Maggie went to the front door of the bar and closed it firmly, locking it top and bottom. Then she rejoined the others.

'You've too big a mouth on you, Patrick,' she said coldly. 'And Eugene, you should know better than to be down here in the public bar at this time of day. Wait until after hours, that's the rule. And Patrick, you're not being much of a lookout, are you? The bloody SAS could be at the back door for all you know.'

'They're not at the back door,' Mooney said gleefully. 'They're either back in England or splattered all over the hills of Armagh.'

He and Finn began laughing. They seemed a little drunk, intoxicated by the success of the joint operations.

'All right, we've had a success; but now there'll be hell to pay for it. It's time you were moving on, Eugene. Maybe you should go to Brian McMullan's house. It's too dangerous to stay in one place for so long.'

'McMullan's place was raided by the Brits yesterday,' Finn told her. 'Fuck knows why. But it's out.'

'Maybe you should head across the border,' Mooney suggested. 'Cavan, or Wicklow.'

'I'm not ready to leave yet,' Finn said. The humour had left him.

'For God's sake, Eugene,' Maggie exploded. 'You're the most wanted man in the North. You can't keep playing the lone hero for ever. It's time things were left to cool down a wee bit.'

'Oh, but I'm not the most wanted man,' Finn said quietly. 'Our friend the Fox is, far and away. It was him that brought that chopper down today, wasn't it? Maybe he should think about heading south too.'

'He can take care of himself,' Maggie said acidly. 'The Brits haven't even figured out who he is yet.'

'They will, Maggie, they will. They figure everything out in the end, the bastards.'

Seeing her look, Finn laughed.

'All right, Mammy, I'll do as you say. I'll head south in the morning. Patrick here can drive me up as far as Derry, and we'll cross the border there, head for Donegal. Maybe I'll do a spot of fishing.'

'And tonight?'

Finn raised his glass. 'Tonight I'm going to sit and have a few drinks to the success of our missions and the overthrow of British arms. *Slainte*.' And he drained his pint.

'And Maggie, open that door, love, will you? People will begin to think there's something wrong if Lavery's isn't open for the evening crowd.'

They checked the weapons again in the disused sewage works. The windows had been boarded up but Early had prised free one board with a crowbar, replacing it after they were inside. Now they were crouched in the musty darkness of the empty building, loading magazines by torchlight. The smell in the place, that damp, unused smell, was akin to the smell in the house where he had been tortured, Early realized. It was altogether fitting that Finn would receive the same treatment here.

But it all depended on speed. They had to snatch the player with a minimum of fuss, get him back there, work on him until he divulged the identity of the Fox, and then set out again to nail the other terrorist. And all this in one night. It could be done, Early was sure of it; but if they bungled the snatch, or if Finn was unexpectedly stubborn, then they could find themselves in a world of shit.

One good thing had come out of the two terrorist attacks that day: Cordwain was totally on board now. Early had felt that the SAS major had not been wholly committed to his plans before, but the news of the downing of the Puma and the subsequent ambush had changed all that.

They had been in contact with Bessbrook. Three had died in the chopper: the pilot, Chandler, and Boyd. Cordwain felt responsible. More importantly, he wanted revenge, and that was good.

'What's the time?' Cordwain asked.

'Eleven-thirty. Things should be calming down in the bar round about now. It's not a Saturday night or anything. At 0200 hours we move in.'

'I know,' Cordwain said testily. 'But what if there's still a customer or two in there, even at that time?'

'We truss them up and lock them in the cellar,' Early replied promptly. 'And remember – Ulster accents all the time. We're trying to suggest this is all part of a feud.'

Cordwain loaded his Heckler & Koch and hung it from his shoulder-sling. He and Early were both dressed in black boiler suits – the preferred dress of players out on a hit. They wore black caps which when pulled down over the face became Balaclavas, and surgical gloves. Their pockets bulged with parcel tape and a metal cosh dangled from a lanyard attached to Early's shoulder.

'How will we make Finn talk?' Cordwain asked. 'He's a hard bastard. We could kill him before he's said a word.'

Early reached in his day-sack and produced a gleaming metal object.

'What the . . .?'

'It's a blowtorch. We'll fry his balls for him and see how he likes it.'

Cordwain was about to protest, but remembering the men who had died that day, he said nothing. Finn deserved whatever was coming to him.

'Grab some kip if you can,' Early advised him. 'I'll keep an eye open.'

Cordwain lay down on the hard floor, eyes open. Early flicked off the torch and they were in total darkness. And silence – they were well away from the road here, in a slight dip screened by trees. The car had been camouflaged and stashed in a small copse off the Monog road, some two hundred metres away, but Early didn't intend to use it. They were going in on foot, to avoid army foot patrols and VCPs as much as anything else, and if Finn caused too much trouble they'd carry him out bodily. They only had half a kilometre or less to travel.

It was a cowboy operation in the worst sense of the word, Cordwain knew that; but with time so short there was little else they could do. Seven men had died that day. If Early and he neutralized both Finn and the Fox, they could be sure that the Regiment, and the Northern Ireland Office, would pull out all the stops to see them out of trouble. That was the idea, anyway.

Cordwain looked at his watch. Midnight. Another two hours to lie there and think. He hated the slack time before the beginning of an op. It was the worst time – once the thing had begun he would feel better. He closed his eyes and tried to doze.

Early was wide awake, peering through a slit below the boards that covered the windows. He could see the odd car passing on the Dundalk road; a white, speeding light through the screening trees. For hours now he had been racking his brains, trying to remember anything he had learned in his time under cover, any seemingly worthless piece of information that might aid them tonight.

Noise was the thing. Everything would have to be carried out in near-silence, to buy time for Finn's interrogation. He and Cordwain would have to move swiftly. Now where in the pub would Finn be hiding? He might have to get that information out of Brendan or Maggie, and did not relish the prospect. Despite all he knew about her, he had to admit there was still a feeling there for Maggie, absurd though it might be. If things had been different . . .

'Fuck,' he growled, but not loud enough for Cordwain to hear him. He had to get that girl out of his mind.

The two hours crawled by. Early knew that Cordwain was awake, but neither spoke to the other. Both knew that tonight was their last chance to even the score, to wipe out their earlier mistakes, and neither intended to muff it.

Finally, Early checked his watch for the fiftieth time, and then crawled over to Cordwain and tapped him lightly on the shoulder.

'It's showtime.'

22

The sky was clouded, so there was no moon. Early and Cordwain made good time, travelling north-west along the triangle of open country between the Dundalk and the Monog roads. There was a farm ahead of them, which they bypassed, causing a restless dog to bark for a few moments. Soon they were in the outskirts of Crossmaglen, in the back of Carlingford Street. Their pace slowed. They pulled the Balaclavas down over their faces and unholstered their MP5Ks, cocking them simultaneously. Then they moved on, Early in the lead, Cordwain following five yards behind, turning every so often to check his rear.

They entered Carlingford Street. It seemed very bright after the darkness of the fields they had come across. The street-lights were glowing amber; the place was deserted. Early checked the time: 0215.

They moved forward more slowly now, taking advantage of every shadow and every possible fire-position. There was no telling what state of alert the locals would be in – and Mooney, Finn's minder – it was likely he was detailed to keep an eye out through part of the night at least.

They halted in the yard at the rear of Lavery's bar. Early knew the place like the back of his hand. He ran to the back door while Cordwain covered the entrance to the yard. It was locked. There was no sound, no light from within, but that meant nothing. He would hear little from the public bar here, at the back, and the windows of the place were covered with heavy curtains.

He produced his lock-pick and knelt down by the back door. Then he began fiddling with the tumblers inside the lock, trying to gauge the pressure and the angle that would make each one click back.

Sweat trickled in his armpits, and the Balaclava seemed to stifle his breathing, but he forced himself to work patiently. There was no sign of Cordwain: the SAS major had chosen himself a concealed position to watch over the yard.

A click, and the tumblers had fallen. Early sighed with relief. He turned the door handle, keeping the SMG trained forward.

The door swung open.

He moved inside. It was darker than in the yard, and he paused a moment to let his eyes adjust.

Cordwain was at the door with him, facing out into the yard. Early tapped him on the shoulder and then pointed wordlessly down the corridor that led from the kitchen. Cordwain nodded.

Early padded down the corridor or hallway that led to the back of the public bar. At the door to its rear he stopped and listened. He could hear it clearly now – several voices talking, someone laughing, glasses clinking.

Fuck! That made things vastly more complicated.

He gave Cordwain the thumbs-down sign for enemy, then held up five fingers – his guess at the number of people in the bar. Cordwain's eyes rolled behind the mask. He joined him at the door.

'After three,' Early whispered.

The door was kicked open with a crash and the two men burst into the room with guns levelled.

'Nobody move!' a harsh Belfast accent said. 'Anybody moves and they fucking die!'

Someone dropped a glass and it smashed on the floor. The rest stood or sat open-mouthed.

Finn was there. Early felt a surge of hatred and exultation that made him grin like a maniac behind his mask. They had him.

Brendan Lavery was sitting with his head in his hands; he looked tired rather than terrified, and obviously the worse for wear. Young Patrick Mooney looked absolutely blank; he'd have to be searched. There were two others, both locals; sympathizers but not active players Early recalled. No sign of Maggie though.

'On the floor, spread-eagled,' Cordwain was telling them. 'Come on – we haven't got all fucking night.'

'Who the hell are you?' Finn asked angrily.

Cordwain slammed the short butt of his weapon into Finn's face. The terrorist fell to the floor.

'You fuckers!' Mooney yelled. His hand reached under his jacket.

Early saw the glint of the pistol barrel and brought up his own weapon. He fired a three-round burst that tore out the man's chest and sent him careering across the room, ribbons of blood sprinkling the walls and floor as he hit the ground. An old Webley pistol was still clutched in his hand.

'Shit!' Early hissed. The gunfire had seemed shockingly loud in the confined space; it was too much to hope that the locals had not heard it – or the army for that matter.

'You bastards!' one of the men was saying. 'You murderers.'

'They're Brits,' Finn said thickly, blood marking his jaw. 'Fucking SAS out for revenge after their wee chopper had a bump. Isn't that right, boys?'

Early felt an urge to shoot him there and then but instead concentrated on trussing them up one by one in yards of parcel tape while Cordwain covered him. Mooney lay with his eyes open, staring sightlessly at the ceiling. The blood had stopped oozing out of his butchered chest with his heart no longer pumping.

'Where's Maggie?' Early demanded of Finn. He was the only one whose mouth he had not taped up.

'Fuck away off,' the IRA man said scornfully.

Early searched him roughly, feeling down his limbs. In the small of the terrorist's back he touched a hard shape, and pulled it out, smiling. A little Walther 9mm handgun, the one he had left behind. He tucked it in a thigh pocket.

'Time to go,' Cordwain said. He was looking out at the square from behind the curtains.

'There's people coming down the street. It won't be long before they're hammering at the door.'

'You pair are fucked,' Finn gloated.

Early lowered his face close to Finn's.

'So are you,' he said quietly.

They dragged Finn through the pub to the back, having taped up his mouth at the last. When he dragged his feet he was beaten with Early's cosh. Finally they were at the back door. They paused before stepping into the yard.

'Listen,' Cordwain said.

They could hear the distinctive warbling sound of Landrover tyres from the square at the top of the street. The army were arriving.

'Time to go,' Cordwain went on.

'No, wait,' Early said. Something was wrong – they had missed something, he was sure of it.

'Come *on!*' Cordwain urged him.

'You go. Get Finn out of here. There's something I want to check.'

'For Christ's sake.'

'Go. I'll catch up with you.' Early turned and re-entered the pub.

He went back to the public bar and, kneeling over Brendan Lavery, ripped off the tape covering his mouth. Lavery yelled in pain.

'Brendan, where's your sister?'

'Leave me alone. Leave us all alone.' He was drunk and slurred his words.

Someone began hammering at the front door.

'Brendan! Are you all right in there? We heard shots.'

'Fuck.' Early began to sweat. 'Brendan, where's Maggie?'

'Toilet,' the man mumbled. He seemed almost comatose with a mixture of shock and alcohol.

The banging on the door began again. There were voices talking outside. One of the men on the floor began to struggle against the tape that bound his arms and legs. Early kicked him savagely until he was quiet.

He rose, and went down to the door at the end of the bar marked 'Ladies' and pushed it open.

A single stall, a hand-basin – nothing else.

He prodded open the door of the stall with the SMG. The toilet-seat was down, and the window above the cistern was open, letting in a draught of night air.

He cursed silently.

That hammering on the door of the bar again. Soon someone with sense would try the back door. It was time to go.

Early sped through the pub, turning out the lights as he left the public bar. He ran down the corridor and then out the back door.

Two men came pelting down the road after him, running out of the square at the top of the street.

'Hey, you!' they yelled.

Early spun, still running, and put a shot over their heads. They threw themselves to the ground and he ran on, into the darkness of the fields beyond the street-lights. He could hear sirens breaking the night quiet of Cross behind him. He kept running.

Finn's face was shining with blood from the blows Cordwain had dealt him in an effort to make him speed up. The IRA man was holding back, trying to delay them both. He knew, Cordwain thought, that he was being led to his death, and at this stage even capture by the British Army was preferable.

Farm buildings looked darkly ahead. If he looked back he could see downhill to where Cross was a tangle of lights. He could hear sirens.

The land ahead was rising gently, a river valley with trees scattered along its bottom. The Monog road was on the height to his left, the Dundalk road on the rise to his right.

He tugged Finn along brutally, wondering what had got into Early. The Lavery woman – was that it? She hadn't been there. In any case, the whole operation was fucked up now. They'd never get anywhere near Cross again tonight – it would be swarming with the Security Forces. They had failed to nail the Fox after all.

But they still had Finn. And Cordwain for one would be glad to put a bullet in the back of his head.

He tugged the IRA man along savagely. Finn was having trouble breathing because of the tape that covered his mouth.

His nose was bleeding, and his eyes bulged like grapes, but Cordwain would not allow him to stop.

The trees were just up ahead. They were out of the town now, into the darkened countryside. Another hundred and fifty yards and they would be at the sewage works. Finn stumbled and Cordwain bent to haul him to his feet again.

A loud crack, startling in the night air. It sounded as though someone had let off a banger.

Cordwain threw himself to the ground beside Finn. A sniper. Christ – it might even be the Fox himself.

Another shot. This time a spray of earth exploded two feet from Cordwain's face. The SAS officer manhandled Finn round until he was lying behind the terrorist as though he were a sandbag. The firing stopped. Cordwain searched the darkness ahead but could make out nothing in the deeper shade under the trees. He cursed aloud, wishing they had brought the NVGs; but they had wanted to carry a minimum of equipment. He was blind, and had seen no muzzle flash. Doubtless, the sniper was now manoeuvring for a better fire-position.

He could hear the sirens wailing back down in Cross. Soon the army would start cordoning off the area. He had to move on.

'Come on, fucker,' he hissed to Finn, and dragged him to his feet. He pushed the IRA man in front of himself as cover and began shoving him forward, up the hill.

They made ten yards, and then Finn threw himself violently to one side, landing headlong in the grass. For a split second Cordwain stood alone.

A shot cracked out, and he was blasted off his feet.

23

Early heard the firing ahead and increased his pace to a fast, ground-eating run. He had heard three well-spaced shots: the mark of a sniper.

Something plucked at the air beside his ear. He felt a thump in his right shoulder and went down, rolling along the ground. Without a pause, he scrambled into a dip in the ground and lay there, panting.

He put up a hand to his shoulder and it came away wet, sticky. The bullet had given him the merest clip, like the slash of a blunt knife. He had not even heard the retort. Was there more than one sniper out there? If so, they were equipped with infrared sights, the bastards.

Cordwain was in trouble – he was sure of that at least. Ignoring the growing ache that ran down his right arm, he began crawling off to one flank, to try to get round the enemy.

Cordwain lay on the grass with the breath rattling in and out of his throat. There were dark shapes moving around him but he could not lift a finger. The high-calibre bullet had taken him squarely in the chest, exploding out his back and ripping his spinal cord to shreds. He coughed, bringing up blood and phlegm. At least one lung had been punctured.

A face bent over him, battered and savaged. It was Finn. Someone else crouched beside him, carrying the long shape of a heavy rifle. Cordwain could not speak.

'Here's a wee present for you, Brit,' Finn was saying, grinning, and Cordwain could feel the cold muzzle of his own weapon placed against his temple.

'Burn in hell, you fucker,' Finn said, and pulled the trigger.

There was a bright flare, like the flash of sunlight on water, and then nothing. The pain and the darkness of the night had gone. Cordwain was dead.

Finn straightened, rubbing his bleeding nose.

'There's another one round here somewhere. We'd better fuck off.'

His companion wore a Balaclava and carried a Barratt-Browning sniper rifle, the bipod extended. With a swift gesture, the mask was ripped off, and Maggie Lavery stood there, looking down on what was left of the dead SAS officer's face.

'I've seen him before. He came into the bar once, I think.'

'Aye, they've been creeping round our heels for weeks. Looks like we're rid of them now though. Come on, Maggie, let's move. We'll head east, and see if we can pick up a car in Monog.'

The pair of them started off, putting their backs to the lights of Cross, and leaving the corpse on the ground behind them.

Early heard the three-round burst of the MP5K, and then the silence. He forced himself not to hurry. At least Cordwain was still firing.

But there was something wrong – something he didn't like. Perhaps it was the sudden, heavy silence after that last burst. It made the firing sound too final – like a *coup de grâce*.

He began running at a crouch along the side of the valley, his eyes as wide as an animal's on the hunt. As soon as he saw the shape on the ground he knew what it was. His stomach turned over. He approached the body cautiously, checked it for signs of life even though the injuries were too massive for anyone to survive. Then he closed the blood-filled eyes and knelt in silence for a second. He had known James Cordwain in the Falklands, when they had both landed on the islands weeks before the Task Force. Now he lay dead on a South Armagh hillside, finished off by his own weapon. He had deserved better than to die in an ugly, petty little struggle like this.

Early rose, and examined the grass about the body. The dew was falling, wetting his legs. It was easy to pick up the trail running east along the floor of the valley; two people, walking abreast.

He started after them, his face filled with murder.

'Did you hear something?' Maggie asked Finn.

They paused. The lights of Cross were a distant glow now, half hidden by the slopes they had traversed.

'No,' Finn said. He was edgy, impatient.

'For fuck's sake, Maggie, that other bastard is still out there somewhere; we can't stand around all night.'

Maggie was stock-still, listening. Though the sniper rifle she bore was extremely heavy, she carried it as easily as if it were a broomstick.

'They were SAS, weren't they?'

'Too right. And they weren't going to get me into any court, either.'

'Lucky for you I had to have a pee, Eugene.'
'Maggie, come *on!*'
They started forward again.

Early stopped, breathing hard. He had heard the voices and had circled round them. Now he was upslope of the enemy, his back to the Monog road. The ground was broken here, covered with crags and boulders. He settled himself in behind one and peered out into the darkness, ears pricked for the slightest sound. His right arm was painful and clumsy, so he held the SMG in his left, steadying it on the rock in front of him.

Something about one of the voices had bothered him. Was it a boy's or a woman's? He couldn't tell – he had only heard them murmuring to each other. They must be close now.

A rattle of loose rock. They were very near, labouring up the rocky slope towards him.

A car came speeding up the road behind him. As it turned he glanced involuntarily at it and caught the glare of the headlights full in the face. The car sped off towards Cross.

Christ! His night vision was shot to shit. He blinked furiously, the after-images swimming before his eyes. The darkness of the night seemed impenetrable, like a blank wall, whereas a few moments before he had been able to distinguish shapes and objects. He had been too long out of the field; he shouldn't have been caught like that.

He closed his eyes, forced his breathing to slow, and listened as intently as a blind man.

Yes, they were closer now, maybe a hundred metres, maybe less. Slightly down to his left. He edged round the muzzle of the MP5K and clicked it on to automatic fire. His vision was not good enough to chance single shots.

Shapes were forming as he opened his eyes again. His eyes were recovering their night vision. He could see two figures walking towards him, one taller than the other. They were barely fifty metres away.

He squinted down the gun barrel and opened fire on the tall one.

The little weapon jumped like a live thing in his hands. Two quick bursts: the classic double tap. He thought he saw one figure go down and switched aim.

Shit! Too slow; the other terrorist had gone to ground. Early crawled out of his fire-position, just as a massively heavy round slammed into the boulder he had been hiding behind. He swore softly. So it was the Fox who was still in action.

He paused and changed mags, then listened. The night was silent again, dark and moonless. But the Fox was using a night-sight – he must remember that.

He began crawling off to the left, careful of every stone, trying to keep to lower dips in the ground.

The sharp retort of another shot. He heard the thump of its impact, then the high whine of a ricochet as it rebounded off rock.

But he had seen the muzzle flash.

Now, you fucker, he thought. I've got you.

With infinite care, he edged over the rocky ground foot by foot, praying that the Fox would be either too afraid or too bloody-minded to bug out. His night vision was improving rapidly: he could see the individual boulders and rocks that littered the side of the hill.

Hoarse breathing, just in front.

He jumped up and fired at the shape he saw moving in front of him. There was a scream, and he threw himself down again, bruising his ribs on a stone. Relief flooded through him.

Got you . . . I got you.

He crawled forward, still cautious, and found a body lying draped over the rocks. He grabbed the hair and pulled the head round.

And found himself looking down at the shattered face of Eugene Finn.

The bullets had shot away his lower jaw; Early could see the tongue poking out into space like a fat worm. He released his grip in disgust and the head dropped to the stone with a sodden thud. Early dragged off his Balaclava and wiped his streaming face with it.

It must have been Finn he had hit the first time – his chest was riddled. He must have been trying to crawl to safety. So that meant . . . A rattle of falling rock off to his right. Early leapt up and sped off after it. He thought he saw a flicker of movement ahead, and grinned to himself. The Fox was running, panicked now.

Something smashed into Early's leg and knocked him off his feet. His weapon went flying and clattered off a rock a few feet away. He hit the ground heavily and screamed. The bullet had hit him squarely in the thigh. He could see broken splinters of bone glistening through his ripped flesh, and the torn material of his boiler suit.

Someone coming. He forced himself to ignore the agony, to draw the pistol and click back the hammer.

There was a roaring in the air, a great thudding noise. A helicopter wheeled over the hillside, its searchlight probing the shadows and lighting up the night unbearably. It was coming east, towards him. Early shielded his eyes.

A figure was silhouetted by the glare of the roving searchlight. It stood over him, rifle in shoulder.

'Dominic,' the voice said, shocked.

He squinted. The helicopter was almost overhead. Its light blinded him and the roar of its rotors blocked out all other noise. He raised his pistol at the silhouette that stood over him and fired. Even when the shape fell, he continued firing. The body hit the ground and twitched as the 9mm slugs ripped into it.

Early heard the 'dead man's click' of the empty magazine at the same time as he saw the face of his enemy, and the mane of chestnut hair that was fluttering in the backwash of the rotors.

He stared in horror at Maggie Lavery's dead face.

Epilogue

Brigadier General Whelan stared out of the window of his office at the rain that was coming down in sheets outside. He sucked on his pipe, but it had gone out. He turned back to his desk.

'Well?' the man in the suit said.

Whelan scowled at him.

'It's a bloody shambles, of course. The last of Ulster Troop left this morning; there are, as of noon today, no SAS operating in the Province.'

'I'm sure the Minister will be happy to hear that,' the man in the suit said, smiling. He was sitting with his briefcase on his lap. He held a manila folder in his hand.

'And this . . . Early chap. What about him?'

'He's in a bad way as I understand – may lose his leg. He's been flown back across the water to recover. The Regiment, funnily enough, is showing signs of standing by him. Usually they drop hooligans like him as though they were hot potatoes. He'll face charges, of course.'

'A sorry business.'

'Indeed. Eight men in one day, and three of them SAS. That's more than the Regiment has lost here in the past twenty years. It's a shame about James Cordwain. He was a good man, if a little flamboyant.'

'But the Border Fox is accounted for.'

'Yes, there is that, I suppose. This man Early shot her. The chopper caught it all on film. An absurdly pretty girl, too. Christ, what a country. Will you have a drink?'

'Thank you, no,' said the man in the suit.

Whelan regarded him suspiciously for a moment, then went over to the corner cabinet and poured himself a whiskey.

'So who is to be my replacement?' he asked sharply.

'General Joseph Waring, from NORTHAG.'

'Joe Waring, eh? Well, he'll do a good job.' Whelan went and stood at the window again, looking out at the grey day. He sipped his whiskey thoughtfully.

'They thought it was war, you see,' he said, without turning round. 'They thought they could make a difference all by themselves: the failing of all young men in all wars. But it's different here. We can go on shooting them and they can go on shooting us till doomsday because it won't make a blind bit of difference. There will always be more young men ready to step forward and fill the shoes of the dead.'

'That's hardly a very encouraging statement, coming from the Commander of Her Majesty's Land Forces, Northern Ireland.'

'Ex-Commander,' Whelan said wryly. He threw back the last of the whiskey and looked at the glass appreciatively.

'Bushmills, lovely stuff. Hard to believe that a country which can make this can have so much hatred in it.'

There was a knock at the door, and then Whelan's aide popped his head around it.

'The car's here, sir.'

Whelan nodded. 'Five minutes.'

He turned to his guest. 'Well, I wish you and the Select Committee well in your inquiry. You should have my official statement within days.'

'And your comments here were, of course, off the record.'

'Of course. Now, if you'll excuse me, I have a plane to catch.' The brigadier general took up his coat and hat, set down his glass, and left without another word.

The man in the suit remained in the room alone a few moments. He stared out the window into the streaming rain, and watched a column of armoured Landrovers file out of the gates of the base to begin their patrol. Just another day in Northern Ireland.